THICKER
THAN BLOOD

by Angela Roquet

Blood Vice
Blood Vice
Blood and Thunder
Blood in the Water
Blood Dolls
Thicker Than Blood
Blood, Sweat, and Tears
Flesh and Blood
Out for Blood

Lana Harvey, Reapers Inc.
Graveyard Shift
Pocket Full of Posies
For the Birds
Psychopomp
Death Wish
Ghost Market
Hellfire and Brimstone
Limbo City Lights (short story collection)
The Illustrated Guide to Limbo City

Spero Heights
Blood Moon
Death at First Sight
The Midnight District

Haunted Properties: Magic and Mayhem Universe
How to Sell a Haunted House
Better Haunts and Graveyards

other titles
Crazy Ex-Ghoulfriend
Backwoods Armageddon

THICKER
THAN BLOOD

BLOOD VICE BOOK FIVE

ANGELA ROQUET

VIOLENT SIREN PRESS

THICKER THAN BLOOD

Copyright © 2018 by Angela Roquet

www.angelaroquet.com

Cover Art by Rebecca Frank

Edited by Chelle Olson of Literally Addicted to Detail

ISBN: 978-1-951603-17-5

For Paul and Xavier,

who make my world go round.

Chapter One

Jenna Hazel Skye, 29, a lifelong resident of University City, MO, passed away Friday morning, January 19, 2018, in a tragic house fire. She was born October 3rd, 1988, the daughter of Antonia Skye, a St. Louis police detective, who preceded her in death.

Jenna graduated from University City High School in 2007 and went on to receive an associate degree in criminal justice before joining the St. Louis police force in 2009, where she served for seven years as a patrol officer within the second precinct. She was promoted to vice detective before transferring to the K9 division, but shortly after was recruited by the FBI and assigned as an agent in a specialized division of the St. Louis field office.

Jenna is survived by her twin sister, Laura, her foster daughter, Amanda, and countless friends and colleagues. In addition to her mother, she is preceded in death by her former partner, Detective William Banks.

A public memorial for Jenna will be held at Mooney Park from 4 to 6 p.m., Thursday, January 25th. The family has requested no flowers and ask that any donations be directed to Project Paws Alive, a non-profit organization that provides lifesaving K9 equipment nationwide.

Well. That was my life in a sugar-coated nutshell.

I would have called foul on the *countless* note, though considering how many jobs I'd blown through in the past year, I supposed the abundance of colleagues made up for the friends I could count on one hand—more like one finger, if I only considered those who knew I was undead but still kicking.

I closed the program and frowned at the outdated picture on the front. It had been taken the day I graduated from the police academy. My blue eyes stared stoically into the camera, completely oblivious to all the fuckery that awaited me in the not-too-distant future.

"You should have seen them." Mandy snorted. Her curls fanned across the white fur throw angled over the foot of my bed, and her skinny legs stretched up the gray duvet cover. She'd shed the wool coat but hadn't yet changed out of the black sweater dress she'd worn to my funeral.

The public memorial was two days off, but I didn't expect Mandy to go. Not everyone had the stomach to keep up such a charade. Speaking of class acts...

"Did Laura put on a good show?" I asked.

Mandy rolled her eyes. "Oh, it was award-worthy, for sure."

I smirked and lay back on the bed beside her, pulling my blond ponytail over my shoulder. In my black tunic and tights, I looked as if I might have been at the funeral with her—and not just posing as a fancy jar of ashes.

I wondered what Laura would do with whatever—or whomever—they'd found to put in my urn. Would she display it on her fireplace mantle? Tell her guests all about me and put on a waterworks show? Would she consider it an improv exercise? The thought made me queasy, so I pushed it away as Mandy snuggled closer.

At this angle, we had a perfect view of the framed photograph above the headboard. The massive sunrise print was the only spot of color in the room, a burst of pink and purple against the shades of gray my little world had been reduced to.

The duke hadn't exactly confined me to the room in his Ladue manor, but he might as well have. There was no one I cared to see in this zip code outside of Mandy, which was convenient since she'd been set up in the room next door. She'd also been tasked with delivering fresh blood to me from the household harem since I refused to feed from the donors. There was no sense getting attached to anyone here.

Mandy chuckled in my ear. "Langford even made an appearance, though his crocodile tears weren't fooling anyone. It was pitiful."

"Ugh. I bet Mathis loved that."

The two police captains were night and day. I'd only served under each of them for a short while before the *incident* that led to my actual death last year, not the staged one mentioned in my obituary.

Mandy laughed again, but it sounded nervous rather than

amused. "Patz was there, too. He kept his mouth shut, but it was all I could do not to take a bite out of him."

I couldn't blame her. Of all the captains I'd worked under, Patz was my least favorite. I'd wanted to take a bite out of him plenty of times myself—even *before* acquiring my fangs. But I didn't really care whether or not Patz was at my funeral. We were just working our way up to the harder questions.

"How are the Bankses doing?" I asked.

Mandy exhaled a long, trembling breath. "Alicia is a wreck. Serena, too. The closing on their house is next Friday. Alicia went ahead and hired a moving company since I had to bail on helping her, thanks to my new *house arrest* schedule. I'm glad that she's going to be closer to Serena."

I hugged myself and resisted the urge to offer Mandy an out. She took offense whenever I suggested releasing her from my harem. I assumed she felt as obligated to me as I did to her, a bond we'd forged long before she began sharing her blood.

"Vin was there, too." Mandy chewed her bottom lip. "He didn't say anything to me, but that's probably because he was too busy pissing himself over Tweedledee and Tweedledum."

Mandy wasn't fond of the werewolf duo the duke had assigned to keep watch over her. I'd spied them out in the hallway the night before the funeral. They were beasts, each at least three times her size, and also the reason we huddled together like girls at a slumber party and spoke in hushed voices—for fear their wolfy ears were pressed against my bedroom door.

There was nothing I could say about Vin without incriminating him or myself. I had a feeling Mandy knew about the mess we'd made—how I'd let him draw my blood to experiment with, and how that blood and research had been stolen by one of his colleagues. Because I clearly wasn't in enough hot water. At least he'd had the good sense not to question my more recent death.

"Lazlo asked if I wanted to stay with him and Collins," Mandy said. A melancholy note entered her voice, and I again felt the tug to offer her a way out of the trap I was caught in.

"Did you tell Collins the truth?"

"He guessed." Mandy's head turned toward me, her voice dropping even lower. "When I went to hug him goodbye, he told me to pat his back if you were okay."

I grinned. "He's always been the smart one."

Mandy's brows knit together, and she looked away from me. "I think he was relieved when I turned down Lazlo's offer."

"It's not you he wants distance from, it's me," I said, lacing my hands together over my stomach.

Collins had done his best to accept what I'd become. He'd even gone through Blood Vice training with Mandy and me.

But I hadn't been honest with him, and that had ultimately ruined our friendship.

Being turned into a vampire was one thing—one very big, very scary thing—but adding myself to the top of an exiled royal's shitlist? Then snacking on our boss's sworn scion? As a member of my blood harem, that put Collins in danger, too.

I guessed we all had to draw a line somewhere. I hadn't quite figured out where mine would fall, but Collins had. It was for the best. Having Mandy's fate in my hands was nerve-wracking enough, and she had her own set of fangs. Besides, Collins would have only complicated matters.

After my last conversation with Roman, the duke had his flunkies confiscate my and Mandy's phones. My line had been canceled, and one of the guards had been assigned to vet all of Mandy's calls. It was just the two of us. Locked in this tense if well-decorated limbo, counting down the nights until the queen announced my replacement sire.

I had a terrible feeling that the duke wanted in the running, but royal scions were more carefully crafted. Everyone thought I was the orphaned, vampling scion of the late Pablo Zajalvo. I was his sloppy seconds, as far as anyone fancy was concerned.

Whoever the queen handed me over to would see the act as a punishment. I'd be a black sheep in a herd of them. After my recent upset in Blood Vice, I had a feeling the queen would be even less likely to appoint me to a decent household.

Someone rapped at the door, and a second later, it opened wide to reveal the duke. He was extra formal tonight, wearing a navy waistcoat over a crisp white shirt. His boyish curls had been combed back and slicked into place with some hair product or another. The look was severe, demanding of respect—a sentiment that had left a sour taste in my mouth where he was concerned. Sure, I respected him. But it was the brand born of fear rather than admiration now.

Mandy and I scrambled off the bed and stood. It was expected in the presence of royalty, but more than that, his visit was alarming. I hadn't seen Dante in almost a week, not since the night he snapped Roman's neck and turned my world inside out.

The sight of him sent a jolt of rage-laced panic through me. My fists clenched at my sides, and I struggled to draw in my next breath.

Belinda, the duke's assistant, and Mandy's wolfy handlers followed Dante inside the room. The two guards had to duck to clear the doorframe, inviting in a healthy dose of claustrophobia along with them.

"Good evening, Ms. Skye." Dante folded his hands behind his back and gave me a placid smile. Then he turned to Mandy, and my stomach dropped. "Ms. Starsgard."

Mandy dipped her head and trained her eyes on the floor.

"Your Grace."

"Allen Cable, head of the St. Louis wolf division of Blood Vice, has formally requested your assistance on a case," Dante said. His eyes darted briefly to me as if to gauge my reaction before he went on. "It is an urgent matter, and I am sending every wolf available to help. It may well be one of the only opportunities you have to stretch your legs over the next few months."

Mandy's breath hitched. I knew she hated being cooped up even more than I did. It was making her crazy, not being able to shift and run free, especially as the moon swelled in the night sky. And I knew how much she admired the Cadaver Dogs. To work a case with them would be a dream come true for her.

But something told me that the duke had ulterior motives for separating me from my only ally under his roof. Mandy seemed to suspect the same.

"I… I can't leave Jenna," she said, shooting me a pained frown. "My blood—she needs me—"

"You won't be gone but a few nights." Dante's focus shifted to me again. "And the household harem is more than adequate, I assure you. I selected each of the donors personally."

"It's okay." I squeezed Mandy's hand and tried to summon a smile. "You should go. It'll be good for you."

Collins had said I was dangerous to be around. No. He'd said I *made* myself dangerous to be around. He was right. And I didn't know how to stop. Half a dozen nefarious plans skipped through my mind, things I wouldn't dare risk if Mandy were around for the duke to use as leverage against me.

Part of me wanted to escape the manor, track down Roman in Denver, and whisk him off to someplace like Spero Heights where we could live happily ever after. But who was I kidding? The duke's detail would be hard enough to ditch, but breaching the BATC facility…by myself… That was impossible.

And then there was the question of whether Roman would even leave with me. For all I knew, he loved his new life as a vampire. I hadn't felt him through our bond since the night he first rose.

Dante cleared his throat and opened an arm to Mandy, directing her to the door. "Mr. Hays is waiting out front with a car as we speak. Belinda will help you pack."

"That soon?" Her pleading eyes met mine, but I refrained from hugging her. I didn't want the duke to see how close we really were. He'd gotten too comfortable taking away the people and things I loved most.

"Good luck," I said, giving her hand one last squeeze before letting go.

Mandy nodded slowly, understanding my reserve. Then she followed Belinda from the room. The two guards trailed behind them, leaving me alone with Dante. He wasn't done with me yet.

I tried to maintain a neutral face and pressed my tongue up under my fangs to keep them in check. For the past five nights, I'd fantasized about all the ways I wanted to kill him. The long, winter hours had occupied my mind with little more than his many gory ends.

But I couldn't. Not with him scrutinizing me from halfway across the room. He was more powerful by far, so at the very least, I'd need the element of surprise—and maybe a solid alibi if I wanted to get away with my retribution, though that was never a priority in my fantasies. Homicidal impulses rarely mixed with reason or proper planning.

"You hate me," Dante finally said, loosing a heavy sigh. "And that is unfortunate, but I do hope you one day realize that everything I have done has been in your best interest."

I stifled a sarcastic huff and folded my hands behind my back, mirroring his stance. He hadn't asked a question, so I didn't feel the need to humor him with a reply. A dry grin tugged up one side of his mouth as he released his arms to his sides, breaking our awkward symmetry. He tucked his hands into the pockets of his dress slacks, but I didn't attempt to copy him this time. I wasn't a complete juvenile.

"I am leaving for Denver tonight to meet with the queen," he said, pausing as if he expected me to pry for details. I ignored the bait. If he wanted me to know something, he could spit it out without forcing cues from me. "I will not be gone long, but I hope you will take advantage of my leave and enjoy the manor in my absence. There is an excellent library in the north wing."

As if a bunch of old vampire books could somehow make up for what he'd done. A week ago, I'd have fallen all over myself and thanked him profusely. But it was going to take a lot more than a library to keep me from ripping his throat out just as soon as I saw an opening.

Dante sighed again and pressed his lips together. "You are nearly as ungrateful as Ursula, and here I am, trying to keep you both safe and comfortable until this mess can be sorted. Why ever do I bother?"

Finally, a question.

"I don't know, *Your Grace*."

He waved a dismissive hand and turned to leave, giving me his back. The opportunity wasn't ideal, but I was desperate and full of loathing. Adrenaline lit up my senses, and instinct drew me across the room in a few long, soundless strides. But somehow, Dante detected me. He spun around, and his hand snatched my neck, my esophagus trapped in the vice of his thumb and forefinger.

"Do not mistake my charity for weakness." His hot breath sliced across my cheek, and I caught a glimpse of fangs as they peeked out from under the curl of his lip. I'd surprised him. The thought was satisfying, even as I struggled to breathe around his grip on my throat.

"Yes, Your Grace," I choked out, locking eyes with him. Dante's pupils widened, eating away at the caramel color of his irises, but I couldn't tell if it was more from fear or anger. He released me without warning and exited the room, slamming the door behind him.

So much for the element of surprise. And so much for my wicked plans. If the duke was leaving, then I couldn't exactly carry out an assault against him. But without Mandy by my side, I was less likely to attempt escape. Sending her away was a calculated move.

Check. But not checkmate.

Chapter Two

Without Mandy to help pass the time, every second was an eternity. I lay on the bed and switched between staring at the sunrise print and the vaulted ceiling. Then I stepped outside onto the terrace and activated my blood vision, using it to spot the guards stationed around the perimeter of the estate in a demented game of *Where's Waldo*. When I tired of that, and my fingers went numb from the cold, I retreated inside and paced the room.

It was barely midnight. Sunrise was seven hours off, and I was already dying of boredom. My stomach pinched, and I realized that the duke hadn't mentioned who or *if* anyone would be taking over Mandy's blood delivery schedule.

Though I knew where the harem was, I hadn't visited it. I didn't know who was in charge, and I figured that Belinda was on her way to Denver with the duke. Which meant that I'd been left with some asshat or other to babysit me.

I paused at the door of my room and considered activating the Eye of Blood again to see if someone warm-blooded waited for me out in the hallway. The gift was draining, as evidenced by my sudden cottonmouth, so I decided against it. Besides, Dante wasn't an idiot. The only time he would risk assigning anything other than a vampire to me was during the day.

Pity. It would have made for a convenient snack.

I cracked the door open and leaned closer, stealing a peek out into the hall. A domed fixture hung from the ceiling, suspended by thin chains. Its light spilled down to the hardwood floor where a muddled reflection shifted, and a faint chirp sounded as if from a smoke detector with a dying battery.

"Looks like I might be on the move," I heard someone whisper. "Put extra eyes on the south wing cameras."

Enjoy the manor, he says. Yeah, right.

As I stepped out into the hallway to get a look at my personal escort, I had a moment of hesitation. Maybe the duke had changed his mind about giving me free rein in his little kingdom. Maybe my failed attempt to off him meant I would be confined to my room without dinner.

The guard gave me a toothy grin as his hand fell away from his ear. He looked maybe thirty—though looks could never be trusted when guessing the age of a vampire. His hair was black and cut short like most of Dante's guards, but there was more…optimism in his expression, as if he were still green enough to enjoy his mind-numbing job.

A small, flesh-colored bud was nestled in the crook of cartilage above his right lobe. The electronic chirp came again. When he noticed me staring, he twisted a dial on the radio at his hip. I spotted a pistol and a small flashlight on his belt, too, before the fold of his jacket hid everything from sight again.

"Sorry about that," he said, pointing at the side of his head. "The hearing in my right ear is shit—too many flashbangs in the military as a human—but if I put that sucker in my left ear, I won't be able to hear anything else."

"Okay…"

"So, where to?" He rolled his shoulders and straightened the cuffs of his jacket sleeves, grinning at me like an oaf. "The harem for a bite? Maybe the gym? Oh! I know…the library." He snapped his fingers. "The big man said something about you liking books, and boy, does he have 'em, let me tell you."

I cocked my head to one side and frowned. Of all the guards, I had to get the Chatty Cathy of the bunch. *Super.*

"Yeah, the library," I said, praying it came complete with a beady-eyed librarian whose death glare demanded silence. "Lead the way…?"

"Murphy." He stuck out his hand, and I accepted it against my better judgment, immediately regretting it when he shook hard enough to rattle my teeth. "Lawrence Russel Murphy the Second," he elaborated as he held tightly to my hand. "But most everyone calls me Murphy. Or just Murph. Sometimes Murphirino or the Murphster—"

"I'll call you whatever the hell you want as long as you don't break my fingers," I said. He let go and took a step back, snorting out a nervous laugh.

"Sorry about that."

"Don't sweat it." I flexed my fingers a few times as the circulation returned.

"Library's this way," Murphy said, pointing down the hall. He waited for me to start walking, and then fell into step beside me, lingering a pace behind. Other than being too gabby—and grabby—he seemed professional, keeping his eyes on me without being obvious and leaving a comfortable buffer of space between us.

More domed light fixtures were spaced down the hallway above the gleaming hardwood floors that smelled of pine and lemon. White baseboards and crown molding outlined the dark-blue walls. Between the doors hung wrapped canvas prints, all displaying the sun kissing the horizon against different backdrops. I'd hardly noticed them when Belinda delivered me to my room last week, but I remembered enough to tell that they'd been changed out.

"You like that one?" Murphy asked, nodding as I paused in front of an orange and blue sunset over a small lake. "It's new. The boss just swapped out most of his collection with fresh takes—two dozen of them, all pretty as a picture." He snorted at his own joke.

"Does he entertain a lot of humans here?" I asked.

"Heck no." Murphy laughed.

"Then why all the sun shots?"

"Why not?" He shrugged. "Humans overcome their disabilities and achieve the impossible all the time. Why shouldn't we get to, too?"

"What do you mean?" I turned away from the canvas and blinked at him. "What disability is the duke overcoming with his limited taste in décor?"

"Oh! You don't know." Murphy shook his head as if amazed. "The boss takes all these pictures himself. Yeah. Lots of guesswork and timers and such. Pretty amazing, huh?"

I looked back at the sunset print in surprise. The images were beautiful, and it was hard not to appreciate them on another level now, though spite kept me from admitting it.

"Sure," I answered dryly before heading on down the hall and ignoring the rest of the prints.

Murphy cleared his throat and pointed at a staircase tucked just inside the arched opening that led into the foyer. "That'll take you to the harem quarters, and it also connects to the upstairs hallway of the north wing, but it's faster to cut across the foyer and take the stairs on the other side."

The foyer was familiar territory. Roman had first brought me here after one of Scarlett's rebuffed harem donors had broken into my house and tried to kill me. If Mandy hadn't been there, she would have succeeded. Together, we'd subdued the fiend, and I'd earned an audience with the duke for the feat, which had resulted in our acceptance into the Blood Vice training program.

The framed photos in the foyer were new, too, but I didn't linger to enjoy them. Not with a vamp as chatty as Murphy watching over my shoulder. I had a feeling he would be reporting every last detail of our exchange to the duke. If I'd been in a better mood, I would have made up some obnoxious and ridiculously long story to tell the guard just for the satisfaction of knowing he'd bore Count Babyface to tears later.

We passed the closed French doors of the duke's office, flanked by two security guards in suits, and entered an arched opening opposite the one we'd just exited. There were stairs tucked inside the mouth of this hallway, too. I'd been up them once before to leave my contact information with the duke's assistant. Belinda's office was on the upper level of the north wing. I hadn't lingered or snooped around after our first meeting, despite not having an escort at the time.

Murphy gave me a wider berth on the stairs, letting me climb several steps ahead of him. I'd thought he was simply being polite until his radio chirped.

"Ascending north stairwell," he said under his breath.

I paused at the landing halfway between the two floors and tossed a glare back at him. "Do you plan on following me everywhere I go tonight? Doesn't the duke have enough camera personnel to keep tabs on his guests?"

The good humor melted from Murphy's face as if I'd hurt his feelings. "The boss just wants to make sure you have someone to show you where everything is. That's all. I'm not here to cramp your style."

"Then why are you relaying my every move to whoever's on the other end of that radio?"

He blinked down at his hip where the device rested. "I'm not relaying *your* every move. We're short-staffed. Two-thirds of the security team went with the duke to Denver. Those of us who stayed behind have to run a tight ship to keep up with the workload. More communication is always better than less."

And here I thought I'd been tempted to escape before.

"Huh. Fair enough." I tried not to look too pleased by the revelation and continued up the stairs.

The upper north wing hallway featured more of the same blue-and-white color scheme and sun canvas prints. Though it didn't run as deep as the south wing. Only two doors graced either wall, and the light fixtures lay flush against the shorter ceiling rather than dangling from chains.

Another hallway split off toward the front of the house. Murphy tilted his head in its direction.

"That way loops around to the staircase near your room." Then he pointed at the door across from Belinda's office.

"The library is right there. Unless you have any other questions, I should get back to my post," he said, giving me a tight smile.

Shit. I *had* hurt his feelings.

"I'm good. Thank you. I appreciate your help finding the library, Mr. Murphy."

"Just Murphy, no mister," he corrected me. "And it was my pleasure." The next smile he offered was more genuine. I tried to return it, but I was out of practice. The strain on my face felt more like a grimace.

Murphy headed for the hall leading to the harem, and I heard him talk to whoever manned the radios one last time. "Taking an early lunch. I'll be back in the south wing in thirty."

Once his footsteps faded, I continued up the north hallway and entered the library. The room was dark, but I quickly found the light switch and flicked it on, illuminating several domed fixtures overhead.

Boredom had motivated my venture into enemy territory, but I hadn't really given much thought to what I'd find. The duke's collection was massive. I took it all in, twisting in a slow circle. Another door farther down from the one I'd entered made me wonder if a wall had been taken out at some point to expand the library into a second room.

Built-in bookcases lined the walls. They were painted the

same deep blue as was seen throughout the rest of the manor and spanned from floor to ceiling, only breaking for the doors and windows. A few feet inside the perimeter of the room, waist-high bookshelves had been placed to create aisles, and more of them divided the room in half, leaving enough space for two large tables on either side. The solid oak slabs were centered in front of two windows, both wide enough to accommodate a cushioned bench between the gaps in the stacks.

I crossed the room and stopped in front of the nearest window, leaning my head against the glass so I could see past my reflection. The moon had dropped behind the web of treetops in the distance, but a swell of artificial light rose up from below, coming from a hedge-lined patio. This stretch of the estate wasn't visible from the terrace off my room.

There was a swimming pool—winterized for the season—and several tables and cushion-less lounge chairs scattered about. Beyond the hedgerow, a vintage greenhouse sat between the patio and a concrete drive that coiled around the north side of the manor. I couldn't imagine Dante hosting a pool party or playing in the dirt and watering plants, but perhaps this area was for the harem's comfort.

I activated my blood vision and picked out a few more guards tucked in the shadows. The property was well-guarded, short-staffed or otherwise. Farther in the distance, a small lake sprawled before the tree line. It was strangely familiar. I knew I'd seen it somewhere before, and from this very angle, but that was impossible. The sense of déjà vu was unnerving.

A disgruntled huff sounded behind me and rose the hairs on my arms. I spun around to find Ursula in the doorway of the library, three books clutched in one hand. Her other was on the doorknob as if she were considering coming back another time. A white sweater dress hugged her thin frame, and matching socks slouched around her ankles. Charcoal gray tights saved the ensemble from the clutches of a winter wedding wonderland.

The Duchess of House Lilith looked every bit as despairing and resentful as she had the night Mandy and I found her, hiding out in a farmhouse outside of Springfield. She shot a withering look at my black-on-black outfit before heading for a corner bookcase.

"Did Daddy let you out for your funeral, vampling? Or didn't anyone tell you that undead fashion has evolved since Drac's reign?" she said before turning her back to me to peruse the shelves. Her red hair was unbound tonight, hanging in elegant waves that almost reached her waist.

I folded my arms over one of the shorter bookcases, resisting the urge to spring on her like I had Dante. The base instinct felt beneath me, but I'd come to recognize it as a side effect of my unfulfilled bloodlust. Hangry vampires were a little more...*bitey* than hangry humans, and I hadn't been feeding especially well lately.

"After twenty years in hiding, what makes you think you know any more about undead fashion than I do?" I asked Ursula, ignoring the way my skin crawled in her presence. She'd sired the vampire who killed me, after all.

I guessed that made her my grandsire, but that bit of trivia wouldn't earn any warm fuzzies if she were to learn of it. As neglectful as Ursula had been of her wayward children, she'd cared enough to risk exposure by sending her half-sired lacky, Annie Miller, to track them down. I had to assume that she'd care enough to avenge Raphael's death, too.

Ursula found a space wide enough to reshelve her borrowed books and then ran her fingers down the adjacent spines in search of something new. "I wasn't in hiding. I was in mourning," she said without looking at me. "And Drac couture was out of fashion even in the nineties."

"I couldn't care less about fashion."

She snorted. "Clearly. Which begs the question, what exactly *did* dear old Pablo see in you?" She pulled a book free from a high shelf and then turned to glare at me.

The duchess had questioned my ancestry the last time we spoke, too. Our conversation had been cut short by the duke but, evidently, she hadn't forgotten where we left off.

"Is being good at my job not a worthy reason?" I asked,

struggling to maintain eye contact with her.

"Good at your job?" Ursula barked out a sharp laugh. "Do you mean to tell me your work with the human police is what caught a reclusive old vamp's attention?" At my alarmed expression, she added, "My cousin told me all about your patchy history. You know, I don't think he's quite convinced you're being truthful either."

I shrugged, but a shiver rocked my shoulders at the same time, defeating the façade. "I'd tell you to ask Pablo yourself, but as you know, he suffered his final sunburn."

Ursula moved across the room in a blur of red and white, stopping a foot in front of me. I gasped and stumbled back a step. My arm lifted instinctively to shield my face, but she caught my wrist. Floral perfume tickled my nose as her pale fingers tightened until my bones protested, and I winced.

"My sire's dead, too, vampling," she whispered as her pupils dilated and her fangs lengthened. "Do you know what that means for a descendant of House Lilith?"

I ground my teeth to keep from panting, but my breath still betrayed me, filling and vacating my lungs at a panicked pace. Of course I knew what it meant. The Eye of Blood was a constant reminder of how I had to hide my true identity. Even within this hidden world.

Ursula's eyelids sagged, and she inhaled deeply. "One taste of your blood, and I'll know exactly who you belong to."

A throat cleared, and both of our heads snapped around to take in Murphy in the open doorway. "I suppose it's a good thing that a regal vampire—like Your Grace—would never engage in such distasteful or unlawful behavior," he said to the duchess.

"I don't need to be lectured by the help," she snapped, then released my arm with an annoyed sniff before turning to the nearest bookcase. I swallowed the scream that had been climbing its way up the back of my throat and rubbed my aching wrist.

Murphy lifted an eyebrow at me. "The harem is presentable if you'd like to continue your tour, Ms. Skye?" He was offering me an escape route that didn't involve ducking tail and running. I was too grateful to be offended.

"Finally," I said, giving him a relieved smile as I cut across the library, eager to put as much distance between Ursula and me as possible. A spot of blood didn't sound half bad either. Maybe it would dampen my impulsive behavior enough to keep me from baiting the duchess into a blood duel.

Now that I knew how eager she was to sink her fangs into me, I was going to have to be extra careful.

Chapter Three

Murphy blew out a tense breath as we exited the north wing and made our way around the hall that led to the harem.

"Thanks," I said, giving him a meaningful look. He accepted my gratitude with a nod.

"Sorry you didn't get much time with the books."

I grimaced. "Sorry I didn't ask you to stick around longer."

"The duchess can be a little…" He pointed at his head and twirled his finger. "Coo coo ca choo. But who wouldn't be after what she's suffered, you know? If my sire bit the big one, I'd be certifiable, too."

"I heard she murdered the princess," I said, watching him from the corner of my eye.

"Nasty rumor." Murphy shook his head, and the skin between his eyebrows puckered. "And I wouldn't repeat it in front of her or the boss if I were you. Offending the royal family will getcha nowhere fast."

We passed several canvases and a trio of windows that overlooked the front lawn and driveway before the hallway turned again, revealing more of the sun prints and blue-and-white color scheme I'd come to expect. There wasn't anything over-the-top about Dante's style. It was well-appointed without being extravagant or wasteful.

Where finding likable things about the duke had set me at ease before, now it irritated me. I wanted to hate everything about him. He'd stolen Roman's humanity and fractured our lifeblood bond before sending him away. Then he'd burned my childhood home to the ground with most of my belongings in it, simultaneously snuffing out my living status.

When—or *if*—I were ever allowed to rejoin Blood Vice, I would have to relocate. And it wouldn't be to Denver where Roman was. No. I'd probably be sent as far away from Denver as possible. Vanessa would see to it.

Murphy cocked his head as we approached a staircase. "That's the one to the south wing."

We passed several closed doors, and then the hallway opened into a gourmet kitchen with stainless steel appliances. Beside the sink was a basket of winter herbs and vegetables, confirming my suspicion about the greenhouse.

A long, quartz counter lined with barstools divided the cooking area from what looked like a hotel lounge. Armchairs and sofas were positioned around two big-screen TVs anchored to opposite walls, and more seating formed a semicircle around a stone fireplace at the back of the room. Massive windows filled in around it and spilled over onto the adjacent walls, making the space look more like an enclosed porch. I could only imagine how incredible the sunsets were to watch from here.

A chorus of cheers drew my attention to one of the televisions where three women and a man were huddled together on a sofa. One of the women violently clicked away on a controller, and I realized that they were playing a video game. Everyone groaned as the cartoon character on screen fell from a cliff to its grisly death.

"Damn it!" the woman grumbled before handing off the controller to the man. She caught sight of Murphy and me and quickly excused herself from the crowd, standing up from the sofa. She couldn't have been but five feet tall, with almond-shaped eyes and straight, black hair that grazed the tops of her shoulders.

"Hey, Yosh. Got someone I'd like you to meet." Murphy beamed at the woman, and her fingers went to her throat to stroke a faint mark near the low-cut collar of her blouse. When she noticed me staring, she blushed and moved her hand away, holding it out to me instead.

"I'm Yoshiko," she said. "You must be the mystery vamp the werewolf girl has been fetching blood for."

"Jenna," I answered with a nod and a tight smile. "Mandy had to leave for a few nights, so I'll be fending for myself until she gets back."

"Oh." Yoshiko's eyebrows lifted, but she didn't ask for more details. "Well, would you like me to arrange for a private visit with a donor, or do you prefer a blood pot to take back to your room?"

"Um…the blood pot, please." I shot Murphy a sideways glance, wondering how pathetic he thought I was for turning down warm blood straight from the vein. I just couldn't risk getting attached to anyone else right now. My heart ached whenever I thought of Natalie, one of my donors from the BATC harem, who had been murdered by one of Scarlett's irrationally loyal rejects.

"Coming right up," Yoshiko said, keeping whatever opinion she had about my selection to herself. She circled the counter and grabbed a clean tray from the dishwasher, quickly loading it with a teapot, a syringe, and a box of bandages. Then she disappeared down a hallway on the other side of the kitchen.

Murphy leaned toward me until his shoulder brushed mine. "No need to be embarrassed. The boss requests blood pots all the time," he whispered in my ear.

"Really?" I made a face. "Why? I would think he'd have a whole tribe of donors all to himself."

Murphy pressed his lips together and sighed. "He's at the right age for a scion, so it's complicated. He doesn't want discord in the harem—donors tend to get all cutthroat with one another if they think they're competing for a royal title and eternal youth."

"Right." I stole a glance at the three humans playing the

video game across the room. They seemed happy and friendly. One of the women propped her feet in the man's lap. I wondered if maybe Murphy weren't giving them enough credit, or if they'd really turn on each other so quickly.

I'd been a human not too long ago, and I liked to think that I wouldn't have thrown any of my friends under the bus for anything so shallow as a crown and an extended shelf life. That sounded more like something Laura would vie for. Hell, she'd probably make a reality show out of the feat.

I smelled blood, and my fangs began to extend before Yoshiko rounded the corner with the tray in hand. She set it on the counter and fetched a knit tea cozy from a drawer, tugging it down over the small pot. Then she added a cloth napkin and a pair of espresso cups.

"Would you like me to deliver it to your room?" she asked with a sweet smile.

"I-I've got it. Thanks." It was a struggle to speak without giving her a flash of my fangs. I didn't want to look any more like a novice than necessary.

"I'll carry it for you," Murphy offered. "I'm scheduled for the south wing tonight anyway."

"Thanks," I said around my fangs again.

Yoshiko's shoulders shivered as he took the tray from her, and her neck and cleavage flushed pink. Her lashes fluttered, and dimples appeared in her cheeks as she looked up at him. Murphy returned her gaze with a wink.

"I'll swing by after my shift ends. You owe me a rematch," he said, eying the crowd gathered around the television. The tone in his voice suggested that he was hoping for more than a video game, but I didn't comment until after we'd said goodbye and began our descent down the south stairwell.

"So...is the harem, like, a free-for-all? Do any of the vamps here have exclusive donors?" I asked. The smirk on Murphy's face told me I wasn't half as sneaky as I fancied myself.

"Yoshiko is my favorite, and I suspect I might be her favorite, too," he said. "But only the duke has any real claim on the house harem. He makes the rules, and Yosh follows them. She pairs the undead staff with suitable donors or fixes their blood pots, and she's good at what she does—so good that the boss doesn't allow requests."

"Requests?" I frowned at him. "You mean you're stuck with whoever she picks out for you?"

Murphy shrugged. "She hasn't had any complaints yet."

"Wow."

It seemed like a strange talent, but somehow, I wasn't surprised to find Yoshiko in the duke's company. He seemed like the type to surround himself with quality help that prevented rather than fostered drama and turmoil.

And there I went again, admiring the creep who had sliced and diced my life.

The radio on Murphy's hip chirped, and he pressed a finger to his earpiece, shoving it in deeper. A frown wrinkled his forehead and tugged down the corners of his mouth as he handed the tray with the pot of blood to me.

"Duty calls," he said grimly. "My apologies."

"Not a problem." I nodded at my bedroom door a few paces away. "I think I can manage from here."

His radio made another noise, and he groaned softly. "On my way now," he said, then hurried down the hallway toward the foyer.

I hoped he wasn't in too much trouble for abandoning his post to play tour guide for me. I hadn't been out of my room for even a full hour, yet I was exhausted and starving. It was likely from all the Eye of Blood abuse. I needed to find a less taxing way to soothe my boredom.

The smell of warm blood wafted up to my nose from the pot as I pushed open my bedroom door. I set the tray on my bedside table and turned to close the door and click on the overhead light. When I faced the inside of my room again, my breath caught in my throat.

The boxes of my most valued possessions that Mandy had salvaged before my house was torched were strewn everywhere. The shade from my mother's fire hydrant lamp was crushed as if someone had stepped on it, and the sweater Laura had gifted me last Christmas hung from a blade of the ceiling fan.

Depleted or not, my blood vision kicked in instantly, and my fangs slid free with a hiss.

If Ursula wanted to know who she was really dealing with, I'd show her.

I threw the door open, nearly ripping it off its hinges, and marched to her room, entering without knocking.

"You've gone too—" The words died in my mouth as the cold night air sucked past me and into the hallway at my back.

The sliding glass door that led out to our shared terrace had been left wide open. Long curtains billowed inside the room, glowing in the thin light of a lamp on the night table. The material whipped into the air, revealing a man dressed all in black.

He looked up at me from where he squatted on the floor, and then I saw Ursula, laid out beneath him, her throat trapped in his hand.

Chapter Four

Ursula's eyes bulged, and she gurgled something at me that I took to mean *help*.

An ugly voice in the pit of my soul rejoiced. *Let the bitch take her suspicions about me to her grave.*

What reason did I have to help her? If we were getting philosophical, I could trace my misfortune back to her just as well as I could blame the duke for it. She'd sired Scarlett and Raphael, after all. If she had done a better job of keeping her scions in check, I'd still be human. Mandy, too.

But then the spark of humanity I still possessed, that instinct to serve and protect, kicked in.

A handful of books on the nightstand caught my eye. Without thinking, I snapped them up and hurled them at the intruder's face. One bounced off his shoulder, but the next smacked his eye and the bridge of his nose. It rocked him back an inch, and Ursula seized it.

The duchess thrust her hips up in a yoga bridge pose. Then she hooked her leg closest to the man around his neck, jerking him down as she slammed her opposite knee into the side of his face.

Something in his eye socket made a horrid crunching noise, and he screamed as he released her throat so he could wiggle free of her thigh hold. By the time he did, I was waiting with the largest of Ursula's library picks.

I swung the book in an uppercut that clipped him under the chin and abruptly ended his scream. His hands groped the air as he stumbled backward, and he snagged the curtain that danced in the wind. The metal rings creaked against the curtain rod, and the material ripped as he used it to right himself.

I was out of books. My hands balled into fists as I waited for his next move. But then a shot thundered inside the room. Blood splattered the curtain, and the man's hand went to his shoulder. I blinked, and then he was gone.

"Your Grace!" Murphy bypassed me to kneel beside Ursula, taking in the red droplets staining her dress. "Are you hurt? Should I call for Harold?"

"I'm fine." Ursula pushed her curls over her shoulder and glared at me as if I hadn't just saved her sorry ass. As if she'd noted my hesitation and held it against me. Then her eyes took in the gory curtains, and she made an affronted noise. "Have someone clean up this mess at once."

"You don't want to taste it first?" I asked, fingering the tacky blood drying in the breeze. Ursula shuddered and gave me another sour look.

"My first use of the princess's parting gift will not be wasted by sucking silver-tainted blood from the drapes. Besides, he was a werewolf."

"You're positive?"

"He reeked of wet dog—though I suppose *you* wouldn't have noticed, what with the little wolf girl you associate with." She ignored my scowl and took Murphy's offered hand, letting him help her to her feet.

"Are you sure you're all right?" he asked again. "Maybe we should take you downstairs where it's more secure."

"Nonsense." Ursula straightened her dress where it had bunched up during the scuffle. "The assassin failed, and now they're wounded. They won't try again tonight." She held up a finger, and her eyes narrowed. "Though I would like a word with whomever let the mongrel slip past the estate perimeter—that is, before Dante has his way with them."

The radio on Murphy's hip beeped, and his jaw flexed. "Evan is dead. All off-duty security personnel are being called in, and the duke has been notified. His entourage is turning around and heading back to the manor now."

"Wonderful." Ursula rolled her eyes. "I'll be in Jenna's room until mine is ready."

"What? Why?" I balked before thinking better of it. I did not want to be left alone with the duchess, especially not after the look she gave me. "I mean…my room was breached, too. It's a complete mess."

Her nose wrinkled with disgust. "Trust me, vampling, I'm not eager for your company either."

When Laura and I were four, and our mother was juggling waitressing shifts and classes at the police academy, we used to spend a lot of time at a neighbor lady's house. Mom didn't have much choice but to leave us with her. It was either that or pick up a second job to pay for daycare, and there were only so many hours that could be squeezed out of one week.

Mrs. Crabtree must have been pushing eighty, but she had enough strength in her old limbs to put the fear of God in both Laura and me. As a retired school teacher, she'd had plenty of experience inflicting corporal punishment via a wooden ruler that she proudly displayed in a cheap china cabinet in her dining room.

Crammed in around the implement was a gaudy collection of floral print tea sets and antique sandwich glass that would rattle anytime Laura or I even so much as walked past the cabinet. Just the faintest clink of china would send Mrs. Crabtree into a frenzy. She'd rise from her knitting chair like Cthulhu from the sea and promise to leave splinters in our asses with her "manners stick" if we didn't stop our tomfoolery.

Not that we were brave enough to ever engage in anything that even came close to tomfoolery in Mrs.

Crabtree's house. We were terrified of her, and rightly so. Mrs. Crabtree didn't make empty threats, and Laura and I had each felt the sting of the manners stick more than once. We weren't angels, to be sure, but we hadn't done anything deserving of the abuse she inflicted. The way Mrs. Crabtree watched us, as if she'd already made up her mind that we were heathens in need of her severe brand of structure and discipline, was insulting and uncalled for.

The Duchess of House Lilith looked at me much the same way. She sat in one of the oval-backed armchairs angled around a table in the corner of my room, sipping a cup of blood poured from the pot Yoshiko had fixed for me.

I'd chugged my own tiny cup of blood like a shot of hard liquor, and then went back for a second before starting in on the task of cleaning up the destruction in my room. It wasn't that I cared about making the place presentable for Ursula. I just didn't want her eyeballing my unmentionables and keepsakes.

It all probably looked like junk to her royal fancypants, and it pained me to accept it, but some things would have to be tossed. Like the shade to my mom's lamp.

"I suppose I should thank you," Ursula said regretfully. I paused in my futile attempt to wrestle the shade's wire rings back in shape and blew a lock of hair out of my face.

"Any idea who's trying to off you?" I asked, refusing to

accept her reluctant gratitude.

Ursula pressed her lips together and set her cup down on the table. "Likely the same monster who murdered my sire." Her stony features softened, and her gaze drew across the room to the closed curtains that hid the wall of windows and the sliding glass door to the terrace. There were four guards standing watch out there last I checked. More paced out in the hallway.

"Someone just have it in for the royal fam?" I said, tucking the lampshade down into one of the plastic tubs Mandy had delivered my things in.

Ursula rested her chin in her hand and sighed. "Only half the households that hold a seat on the Vampiric High Council."

"Only half?"

Her eyes landed on me again and narrowed. "Careful, vampling."

"But you're so pleasant," I said, batting my lashes in mock innocence. "How could anyone wish harm on such a saint."

"I don't need your pretense, but I also demand a certain degree of respect. I am your noble superior," she hissed, unfolding her legs as if preparing to launch herself at me.

"Of course, Your Grace," I said with less venom.

I was being rude and reckless, which meant I needed more blood, but the pot was near empty. Sharing my room and my dinner with someone I despised had done *wonders* for my mood.

I went to the door, hoping I might convince someone in the hallway to fetch another pot, but a commotion outside sent me back a step. A second later, the door flew opened.

"Ms. Skye," the duke greeted me in a tight voice. His eyes were wild, and they searched the room while darting back and forth to me.

I retreated a few steps, giving us both space until he felt comfortable enough to enter the room. Murphy stayed in the doorway behind him. When I caught his attention, I tapped the teapot on my night table, and he nodded before whispering something to another guard in the hall.

Dante went to Ursula, taking her hands in his as she stood.

"I'm fine," she said before he could ask. "Truly. Your little pet project over there helped fend off the brute." She tilted her head in my direction, and the edges of my vision tinged with red. *Pet project?*

"Is that so?" Dante sounded skeptical.

"She bludgeoned him with your first edition copy of *Blood Customs*," Ursula said as if she were tattling on me. With the way the duke frowned at me, maybe she had.

"I meant for you to read the books, not vandalize them."

"Sorry." I held up my hands. "I would have preferred a

gun, but I'm not allowed to carry one here."

"And you will not be allowed until your wrathful resentment has passed," the duke said.

"Maybe I wouldn't be so *wrathful* if you hadn't sabotaged the life I worked so hard to piece back together after—after my sire died." My face flushed, and I hoped I looked more angry than guilty. I bit my tongue, silently cursing myself for coming so close to slipping up and confessing that I'd been murdered, by one of their own no less.

"Your Grace," one of the guards called from the doorway. He pressed a finger to the radio on his belt and gave the duke a guarded expression. "We have unexpected company."

"Well, tell them they need to make an appointment." Dante's jaw flexed as if he couldn't believe the guard would bother him with such a trivial thing at a time like this.

"I would, sir, but they're council officials."

Dante swore under his breath and rubbed a hand over his face. Then he turned to me. "Stay here with the duchess and do not let anyone but me into this room until I return." He left in a hurry without another word, locking the door behind him.

"Council officials?" I blinked at Ursula, hoping she might have more to say about what that could mean.

"Don't look at me." She plopped down in the armchair

and scooped up her cup of blood. "I told you. At least half the council. I've been out of the loop for twenty years, so it's hard telling which of those pompous scoundrels is at the top of the heap right now."

"How many households are we talking about here?" I asked.

"Two hundred, give or take."

My eyes bulged. "So a hundred potential suspects?"

A bitter laugh escaped her. She finished her blood before replying. "Going into hiding doesn't sound like such a bad idea now, does it? Thanks for screwing that up for me."

"Take it up with the duke. I was just following his orders."

I ground my teeth together as I thought of the all things I wished I could thank *her* for screwing up for *me*.

"But you enjoyed bringing me in, didn't you?" Ursula cracked a scathing grin at me. "Was I a suitable consolation prize for being dismissed from Scarlett's trail?"

"Not even close."

Her smile grew sharper. "What is it you think you have to prove, vampling? What is it you're after?"

"Justice." The word sounded more honorable than revenge-tinted, but I tasted the lie in my mouth.

"Justice?" Ursula's eyebrows shot up. "And who are you to decide what justice is? What justice do you suppose should befall a vampling who has fed from her superior's pledged scion?" At my shame-faced scowl she added, "Don't be so quick to dole out justice when you've been lucky enough to escape the brunt of it yourself."

A soft knock at the door ended our stare-off. I crept closer, remembering Dante's order not to let anyone in, but then Murphy's muffled voice reached my ears.

"It's just me," he said. "And a pot of B-positive."

I unlocked the door and cracked it open to accept the pot. He hadn't brought a tray with him, but I suspected he'd skipped it to keep a hand free for his gun.

"Thanks," I whispered, stealing a quick glance down the hall where several guards stood near the entrance to the foyer.

"Better stay put like the boss said." Murphy turned his back to me and trained his eyes on the opposite end of the south wing, keeping watch where the others weren't.

"Will do." I gently closed the door and turned to refill my cup on the night table, pausing when Ursula cleared her throat. She held up her empty cup.

"Guests first, little vampling. Goodness, I learned that much as a human."

My fingers tightened on the handle of the pot as I crossed the room. I imagined opening the lid and sloshing the blood at her *Carrie*-style, though her white sweater dress was already ruined. The thought was amusing, but it wouldn't end well.

And I needed the blood if I was expected to tolerate her until the duke's meeting with the council visitors was over.

Ursula watched me closely as I poured her drink. Her smug grin suggested that she knew exactly how much I hated catering to her, and she was loving every second of it. I hadn't tracked her down for the duke so we could have bloody tea parties. This was all wrong.

There were dozens of guards in the manor. How the hell had I ended up trapped in this room, babysitting the duchess? And why did I suddenly feel as if I were stuck in quicksand?

Ursula's grin widened as she watched me fill my own cup and sit down on the edge of the bed. It was unnerving. Whatever dark thoughts rolled through her head, I didn't even want to know.

"You have blood in your teeth, *Your Grace*," I said, tilting my cup at her in a sardonic toast.

Her eerie grin didn't waver. "Mind your tongue, vampling, or it will be *your* blood that stains my teeth next."

Chapter Five

When the duke finally returned to my room, his haggard expression left me less than relieved. He'd shed his waistcoat and undid the top button of his white shirt, and though his hair was still shiny from whatever he'd put in it earlier, its hold was slipping. Random curls poked free, made worse by the way he nervously raked his hand over his head.

"Show Ms. Skye to my quarters," he said over his shoulder to Murphy. "And have my morning blood brought there, as well."

"Uh…" I didn't know what to say.

A few hours earlier, I'd made a move on him—and not the sexy kind guys usually preferred. The kill 'em with bare hands variety. And now he was inviting me into his room? All because I'd used a fancy book to slug the creep who tried to whack his twatwaffle of a cousin? I wasn't sure if more scolding or congratulations awaited me.

Understanding lit Dante's eyes as he noted my confusion. "I need a word with my cousin, and her room is not ready just yet. I will be with you in but a moment."

"Yes, Your Grace."

Murphy waved his hand to encourage me along, and I left the room with him, still confused. We passed several guards, but once we were out of earshot, I turned to my only potential ally.

"What the hell is going on?" I rasped under my breath.

Murphy shook his head. "I'm not in the business of asking questions. I'm just here to help pretty ladies find the library and to keep bad guys from crashing the party."

My eyes narrowed skeptically. "And you don't ever overhear anything useful?"

"Nope." He pointed to his bad ear. "Only the stuff I'm meant to hear. I'm good at my job that way." His face crumpled, and he shot me an apologetic frown. "Sorry about earlier—leaving you alone like that. I should have told control to call in someone else to check the exterior posts and stayed by your side."

"Hey." I touched his arm. "I was a Blood Vice agent before this Rapunzel gig. I can take care of myself."

"Yeah, but I knew you were unarmed. And then the duchess was under attack." He shook his head. "It all happened so fast, and if I'd stayed put, you wouldn't have had to go to such lengths to protect her."

Yeah, I'd really gone to some lengths. I resisted rolling my eyes and patted his arm. "You showed up just in time, and you shot the creep. I think you did great."

"I appreciate that," Murphy said, though it didn't sound like he believed me.

We passed the stairwell and entered the foyer where there

were now eight guards on watch—two at the doors to Dante's office, two at the front doors, and two each at the mouths to the north and south wings. Total overkill, but after the events of the night, who could blame the duke for beefing up security?

Murphy directed me down a hallway that curled around the office and opened to a secondary foyer mirroring the one at the front of the house. It was narrower but furnished with the same leather benches and more sun shots. Another pair of French doors marked the entrance to the duke's private quarters, and two more guards were stationed on either side. They opened the doors for us without question.

Inside, Murphy clicked on the lights. Then he pressed a button on his radio and asked a guard in the harem to have Yoshiko fix a pot of blood while I scanned the room, taking in the quiet luxury and the earthy color palette.

The duke's quarters were more spacious than mine or Ursula's, but not by much. The windows that enclosed the back half of the room were split by a stone fireplace. Two armchairs and a side table were centered in front of it, and I realized that the harem's lounge must be directly above.

A bit closer to the interior of the house, the leather-wrapped headboard of a king-sized bed was pushed up against the northern wall, flanked by simple, modern nightstands. On one sat a long-necked reading lamp and a stack of books, and on the other, a digital clock that doubled as an electronics charging station. A phone and a tablet were docked in it, and if not for Murphy's presence, I wouldn't have been able to resist snooping.

Who did the Duke of House Lilith keep on speed dial? I wondered.

Across from the bed, a Victorian armoire sat between a pair of closed doors. The piece of furniture looked more intricate and dated than anything else I'd seen in the manor. Ornamental molding lined the paneled doors, three in all, and encircled the full-length mirrors fixed to them. The glass was foggy and tarnished at the edges, giving the piece a nostalgic charm.

"Pretty, ain't it?" Murphy said. "I think it must've belonged to the boss when he was human, but he don't talk about the past much."

I stepped in front of the armoire and looked at myself in the mirrors, trying to picture how I might have appeared in the mid-nineteenth century when the piece was made. When Dante was made. He'd worn a Civil War uniform to the queen's All Hallows' Eve ball, though I wasn't sure if it was a costume or authentic. Authentic would suggest that he'd fought for the Union as some high-ranking official.

I touched the handle of the armoire and considered opening it. Maybe I'd find the uniform inside. Maybe I'd find some other deep, dark secret of the duke's that I could use to make him suffer, something I could take away like everything he'd stolen from me.

"Oh! Blood's here," Murphy called out, halting my meddlesome plans.

I turned around just as Yoshiko entered the room carrying a tea tray set with a pot and two espresso cups. She'd changed out of the casual lounge clothes I'd seen her in earlier and now wore a sleek, black pantsuit. The tired strain in her expression made me wonder if she'd been tasked with delivering blood to the duke's council guests, too.

"Jenna, right?" she said with a halfhearted smile. I nodded as she slipped past me on her way toward the fireplace. "You're in for a special treat. We reserve the richest blood for the duke, and this batch came from two donors who have been on an offal and green juice diet for the past week."

I stuck out my tongue in disgust but quickly reeled it back in when Murphy gave me a chastising glare. Yoshiko left the tray with the blood pot on the table between the two chairs before cutting back across the room.

"Enjoy," she said sweetly before giving Murphy a wider smile and exiting the room.

"It's not like you can taste the offal or greens in their blood," he said once the door had closed behind Yoshiko. "It's just heartier and more filling when they eat food with extra iron and vitamins and such."

"Why not just take a supplement?" I asked.

"They do that, too. But getting what they need through diet is more natural and healthier. The harem donors give a lot of blood, so Yosh does her best to take good care of them."

I shrugged and made my way over to the blood pot, breathing in the warm aroma. It smelled nice. The only time I'd drunk any extra fancy blood was at a house party Roman had taken me to. It had come from a harem for hire called the Blood House Geishas, and it was so amazing that I'd made an absolute fool of myself. I liked to think that I was a bit tamer now.

"Maybe you should wait for the boss," Murphy suggested as I filled one of the espresso cups.

"No need." Dante entered through the French doors behind him. He untucked his white dress shirt from the waist of his pants as he crossed the room. Then he took the cup of blood out of my hand as if I'd poured it for him. The prick.

"You're welcome," I scoffed as he threw the drink back and set the cup down on the tray.

"No, my dear, *you* are welcome." He began unbuttoning his shirt as he turned away from me. "I do not share my pot of morning blood with just anyone. Please, help yourself while I change."

Murphy waited by the entrance, looking entirely too comfortable as the duke stripped out of his formal attire. "Would you like me to take that to the laundry, boss?" he asked.

"You always go above and beyond, Mr. Murphy." Dante tossed the shirt to him and then opened one of the doors beside the armoire. From my vantage point, it looked to be a closet. Dante stepped inside, and a moment later, his pants soared through the air. Murphy caught them and draped them over his arm on top of the shirt.

"Anything else?" he asked, shooting me a cautious glance. I was sure my homicidal urges toward the duke weren't a big secret around the manor.

"That will be all. Thank you," Dante called from the closet.

Murphy dipped his chin in a farewell nod to me. He slipped out the French doors just as Dante reappeared in the room. The duke wore a gray, long-sleeved Henley and a pair of drawstring pants. The look reminded me of the first time I'd met him and how naïve I'd been, thinking he'd solve all my problems.

Dante blinked down at the tray and the clean cup beside the blood pot. "My invitation was sincere."

I snapped out of my gawking daze and poured myself a drink, refilling his cup while I was at it. I didn't need another lecture like I'd gotten from Ursula.

Dante picked up his cup, tapping it gently against mine before drinking it slower than his first. He stared out past the sea of windows around the fireplace to the lit patio tucked between his room and the north wing. Three guards were stationed around the covered swimming pool. I spotted another two farther out on the lawn between the manor and the lake in the distance.

"This manor has never been breached before tonight," Dante said, almost as if to himself.

"I heard you lost a guard."

"We lost two, and another was badly injured." He set his unfinished blood down on the tray and held out his hand toward the armchair in front of me. "Please."

I circled the chair slowly and sat down without taking my eyes off him. After our violent exchange earlier in the night, there wasn't much comfort to be had between us. I waited until he took the chair opposite mine before taking a timid sip of the blood.

An involuntary moan echoed inside the cup, and Dante gave me a knowing grin.

"You are welcome," he said in a tone that mocked my prior rudeness and set my cheeks on fire.

"I've had better."

"So I have heard." The heat in my face spilled down my

neck and into my chest and only spread further as he went on. "I have been told you sampled much worse, as well. Of the *bovine* variety." He shuddered.

"I didn't think you brought me here to discuss our blood preferences."

"No." He laughed. "But I am sure you can guess the topic on my mind."

I set my cup down next to his and folded my arms. "An assassin and an unscheduled council visit all in the same night—and so soon after you left. Coincidence? Or does everyone enjoy your company as much as I do?"

Dante's perpetually sympathetic brows dropped into a flat line that shadowed his eyes, and his jaw flexed. "Do not forget whose home you are currently a guest in."

"I wouldn't be a guest here if you hadn't burned down *my* home," I said, grinding my teeth as I shot him an unpleasant smile.

"You ignorant, ungrateful child." He shook his head and leaned back in his chair.

"Ungrateful?" I snapped, ignoring the *ignorant* and *child* bit of his insult. For now. "Are you suggesting I should have thanked you for what you did?"

"It would be nice, yes. I saved you from a great deal of trouble."

"You ruined my life! How was that saving me from

anything?"

"Very well." Dante clapped his hands together and leaned forward, resting his arms on his knees. "Let us get the trivialities of your woeful predicament out of the way first, shall we? I will even give you the benefit of assuming that you would have somehow avoided drawing suspicion with your dusk-to-dawn schedule, your constant refusal of dinner invitations, or your aversion to silver.

"In twenty years—or even thirty—when your mortal flesh would have no doubt begun to show signs of deterioration, how did you intend to explain your youthful beauty? Your inner circle's awareness of your condition aside, what did you plan to tell acquaintances and colleagues?"

I didn't expect him to humor me with an honest conversation, and I was unprepared for the question. Truthfully, I hadn't given it much thought. Getting by day-to-day—or rather night-to-night—had been challenging enough.

"I had decades to figure that out." My face burned hotter as I searched for a better answer. "There are some really advanced facial creams on the market—and hair can be dyed, *obviously.*"

Okay. Now I sounded like Laura. Dante's lips curled downward into an unimpressed scowl.

"And do these fancy moisturizers also extend your life expectancy? What happens when you surpass your hundredth birthday and continue to look the way you do presently?"

"My hundredth birthday is a long way off. You could have given me more time." My vision blurred, and I blinked back hot tears.

I didn't care how sound his reasoning was. My life was over, and even the new one that I'd begun to build in this secretive world of immortals was out of reach. What would become of me now?

Dante exhaled a long, pitying sigh. "I allowed your wolf girl to gather your most valued possessions, and I have opened an account on your behalf, where I deposited more than enough to cover your financial losses."

"You opened an account in my name?" That was news.

"It is under my company umbrella at a privately-owned vampiric bank. For now, you are just an ID number, but once your sire is appointed and you have your new last name, we shall go in together to amend the account information."

I narrowed my eyes at him. "Why didn't you say something about it before now?"

"You have been here all of a week. The account was set up two nights ago, after my appraisers submitted their findings. I would have mentioned it before leaving for Denver, but you were not in very a talkative mood." He lifted an eyebrow, daring me to deny it.

"And my job with Blood Vice?" I wasn't about to let him

off the hook that easily. My loyalty and trust could not be bought, and I still felt violated and broken. Mostly over Roman, but I was betting the duke didn't have a fix for that one. That I'd been the one in the wrong didn't make it any easier to accept.

"What about your job with Blood Vice?" Dante countered.

"Am I still an agent? Will I be reassigned somewhere else now that I'm ruined for St. Louis?"

"That depends on your sire and what they decide is best for you." I rolled my eyes, earning a snort from him. "This is what you asked for, and from the queen, of all people."

"I wanted someone to show me the ropes—not a tyrannical babysitter who controls every aspect of my life."

A small grin hitched one side of Dante's mouth as if he thought that was *exactly* what I needed. "Then you should have requested a tutor. Now,"—he cleared his throat—"shall we get on with the more pressing matter at hand?" I glowered at him, but he met my ire with one of his more charming smiles. "Oh, come now, Ms. Skye. If you miss your career in law enforcement so much, this may very well cheer you up."

"I somehow doubt that, but please, tell me more," I said, unable to keep my sarcasm in check.

"I intend to." Dante paused to take a sip of blood before circling back to the real reason he wanted to speak with me.

"House Lilith has suffered a great deal in recent years, and I fear the root of this suffering has come from a source within our inner circle. Last week, after Ursula's...um—"

"Capture? Arrest?" I offered.

"*Homecoming*," he said, giving me a pointed look, "I contacted the queen, and she informed the Vampiric High Council the next evening. However, she did not reveal to them where we were keeping the duchess until her hearing."

"Why not?" I asked, though I suspected the answer had something to do with their status.

"The council can be quite indecisive when it suits them, and having a royal prisoner in their clutches would grant undue leverage over House Lilith. They could keep her locked away for months, possibly years until they agreed on a date and location for the trial. In the meantime, they would use her captivity as a bargaining chip to sway the queen's favor. Such behavior cannot be tolerated if the royal family is to stay in power."

"Is that why they were here tonight?" I asked. "Because they found out where the duchess was being kept and wanted to take her into their custody?"

"Yes." Dante cupped his chin in his hand and frowned.

"Do they have the right to do that?"

"Only if the accused's place of holding is compromised—if they attempt escape or are assailed."

"I take it an assassination attempt falls into that category?"

Dante nodded slowly, and we both fell under a spell of quiet contemplation. I tapped my nails on the table between us and then fingered a droplet of blood that had escaped my cup.

It was clear that the duke didn't know how the council had discovered Ursula's whereabouts, but I wasn't sure what made him think I would know anything about it. I'd spent the last week hiding out in my room, with no phone or internet access to speak of. Detective work of this caliber, with so little to go on, just wasn't possible. I was betting not even with a blood sacrifice to Holmes, Tracy, and Poirot.

"So…the real questions you want answers to…" I held out one hand and ticked them off on my fingers. "How did the council find out where Ursula was being kept? How did they find out about the assassin so quickly? And, most importantly, were they involved with the attack?"

"Precisely," Dante said.

"Here's one other I'd like to know," I said, straightening in my seat. "How did you get them to leave here without the duchess?"

"I convinced them that you would protect her."

"*What?*"

He shrugged. "You defended her from the assassin, and

you saved the queen's life. How could they deny your ability?"

"That's not the—you can't expect—" I choked out a nervous laugh. "So, what? Am I, like, her bodyguard now?" I didn't miss my career in law enforcement *that* much.

"Until the hearing has concluded, yes," Dante said. "Don't look so disappointed. Protecting a member of the royal family is considered one of the highest honors for a Blood Vice agent. It will look impressive on your résumé—should your future sire allow you to apply for a position at another field office."

I put my head in my hands and groaned. "Please tell me this trial isn't months or years away."

"The council has scheduled it for Friday." He sighed and finished off his cup of blood.

"That's...soon."

I couldn't say that it displeased me, but I wasn't thrilled about being trapped in a room full of bloodthirsty black hats either. I'd done my best to stay off the council's radar, but now the duke had turned me into an obstacle in their path. That changed the game.

"The council wants this matter resolved before Imbolc," Dante said. "They do not wish to risk the queen publicly recognizing and accepting Ursula before they have the opportunity to crucify her."

"They sound like a friendly bunch."

"Savages," he grumbled. "We have so little time to prepare, but I suppose they were counting on that if they could not hold Ursula themselves and use her to their advantage."

I tried to recall what I'd learned about the vampiric court system from my training at the bat cave. "What exactly is she being accused of?"

Dante's jaw tightened, and a tendon in his neck flexed. "The death of her sire, among other wrongdoings." With his eyes boring into mine, I couldn't find the nerve to ask if she was guilty. But I did consider what I knew of the rest of House Lilith.

Sweat dampened the back of my neck as I tried to find an inconspicuous way to ask if Kassandra, the duchess who had orchestrated the recent attack on the queen, would be at the trial.

I was a royal bastard posing as a low-born, orphaned vampling. When Raphael died his true death, he inadvertently passed on the Eye of Blood, a gift unique to House Lilith. So when I'd bitten Emma after she attacked the queen, I quickly discovered that she was an illegitimate scion of Kassandra's.

I, of course, couldn't share that information without condemning myself. But since Emma's blood had been used to save the queen—and since the queen theoretically possessed the Eye of Blood, too—I had to wonder if

Kassandra was still in the royal family's good graces.

"What is it?" Dante asked. He eyed me hopefully. There had to be some way I could work around my secrets without spilling them all over the place.

"Was the culprit behind the queen's attack apprehended?" I asked. Dante's expression hardened, but he answered openly.

"The assassin's sire was found dead. Lord Kincade was taken into custody, and he and his entire household were questioned. Vigorously. But no one could tell us anything of worth. The council has forbidden them from pledging future scions to Blood Vice, which in turn means they shall never hold a seat at the table, something House Kincade was well on their way toward before this catastrophe."

I nodded slowly. "So there's a good chance Emma was working for someone else. Could the hit on Ursula be the work of the same person or persons?"

"The royal family has many enemies, but I suppose it is possible." Dante watched me with unblinking persistence as if he were waiting for me to get to the point.

"I've heard about the Eye of Blood," I said, waving my hand as if the thought were only just occurring to me. "Did the queen see anything useful when she drank from Emma?"

"I am afraid the queen was too near death to open her Eye of Blood at the time." His chin tilted up, and a damning light sparked behind his eyes. "But you bit her too, did you not? What did you see, Jenna?"

My breath rushed out in a feverish whisper of a laugh. "House Zajalvo doesn't have any special gifts that I'm aware of." I tore my eyes away from his and reached for my cup of blood, flinching when his hand closed over mine.

"I found Zajalvo's scion nights ago. Dead." His voice dropped low and soft, laced with a threat that he didn't have to spell out. "It was a clever ruse, I will give you that. But we both know you did not engineer it on your own."

Roman. I screamed his name through our blood bond. If he could hear me at all, he had to know the danger he was in. My ears rang in the silence that followed, and a chill settled in the pit of my stomach. I swallowed and met the duke's gaze.

"What do you want from me?"

The inner corners of Dante's eyebrows drew up, generating the sympathetic pretense he was so good at. "Which one was it, Jenna?"

I knew what he was asking, and there was no lying this time. Not if I wanted to keep Roman from a more permanent death. I took a deep breath and signed my death warrant.

"Raphael."

Chapter Six

Dante released my hand, and I brought the cup of blood to my lips. It had cooled, and it did little to soothe the nerves that had set my body to vibrating.

My eyes searched the wall of windows. There had to be a sliding glass door tucked among them somewhere. Not that I'd make it far with all the guards swarming the property. Still, I'd put up a fight if it came down to it—though part of me had to believe Dante had other plans if he already knew I was a fraud. The muted horror that stretched between us suggested that he hadn't considered Ursula's exiled scions until just now, and that maybe I should have kept my big mouth shut.

"And his true death?" Dante asked as I cradled the empty espresso cup in my lap.

"Last June. I was working for the St. Louis PD, and my partner and I had been assigned to a sex trafficking case."

"The Scarlett Inn." He nodded, putting the pieces together for himself.

"We were watching a building someone had tipped us off about. It was just before dawn." I pressed my lips together and forced my eyes up to meet his. I couldn't botch this part of the story. I'd already endangered Roman—I couldn't do the same to Mandy. "Raphael arrived, and we followed him inside. He killed my partner…and then he tried to escape, but I followed, and he bit me—" I touched my neck, and a shiver rolled up my spine. "I woke up that night in the morgue."

"Then how…" Dante frowned disbelievingly, but I just blinked and willed myself to think innocent thoughts. "Was he badly injured?"

"I filled him with lead right after my partner did the same, so I imagine."

"His blood ran freely and in close proximity to you."

"Close proximity?" I scoffed. "He mauled me like a rabid dog."

"And you were outside at this point?" Dante asked.

"No." I wasn't stupid enough to contradict the police report. The duke would have seen it after Blood Vice took over the case. "I died in that basement. Bled out just a few feet away from my partner."

He hummed thoughtfully. "So it is to be assumed that he fled the building, and dawn claimed him before he could find adequate shelter?"

"I don't know. I guess?" I shrugged one shoulder and tried to push the image of Mandy's shadowy wolf soaring across the warehouse basement from my mind.

"And how did you discover his name after rising?" Dante asked. I wasn't sure if he was being skeptical or genuinely curious how such a freak accident could occur.

"I was put on leave, but I continued investigating the Scarlett Inn—off the books," I said truthfully. "That's how I found Mandy. She was looking for the inn, too. She'd escaped but came back to free her friends. I know my way around a sketchpad, and I drew Raphael's picture."

"And your wolf identified him?" Dante leaned closer. He was buying it, but I'd included enough of the truth to make it stick.

"She did," I confirmed. There was no sense crediting Roman with the revelation. The less the duke assumed my late lover knew, the safer he would be.

"You are an artist. I didn't realize." It almost sounded like praise, until he added, "I should like to see this sketch."

"Well, that's the funny thing about house fires." I didn't put as much bite into the accusation this time. Nothing either of us said could undo the crime, and in light of more recent events, it had become the least of my worries.

"That is regrettable." It was the closest thing to an apology the duke had offered me. "I will have someone pick up a new sketchpad. You will draw your sire again—for me— just to be sure your wolf was not mistaken."

"*Could* it have been someone else?" I asked. It seemed unlikely that Roman would misidentify the brother of a potential sire who had spent years torturing him until her exile. "Do any other houses have the Eye of Blood?"

"Not that I am aware of, but Ursula's progenies were quite unlawful to be sure. A bastard scion—pardon my Romanian—is not entirely out of the question, and their death could have just as well passed on the birthright."

"Speaking of…" I swallowed, wondering how well my next confession would go over. "The queen's assailant was not a scion of House Kincade."

"I feared as much." Eager wrath widened his eyes. "Tell me who sired the fiend."

"Kassandra."

Dante's hands closed into fists. He brought one up to his face and pressed it over his mouth. He was angry but not as surprised as I expected him to be. "You are absolutely certain?"

"I saw her through Emma's blood. She arrived at the All Hallows' Eve ball right after." The memory was vivid in my mind, and it brought with it the taste of her traitorous scion's blood on the back of my tongue. "Is there some reason Kassandra would want the queen dead—fancy headgear aside?"

Dante grimaced as if he weren't sure he wanted to answer the question. Airing family laundry was not becoming of a royal scion, but technically, I *was* family.

"I believe she may fear that Lili intends to take the prince to her forever rest," Dante said reluctantly. "As Lilith did with

Adam before our time."

"But if the queen were to die before taking her forever rest, then the prince—your sire—would assume control?"

Dante nodded. "And with Morgan's death and Ursula's self-inflicted exile, the council would require little convincing to permit Alexander to take Kassandra as his queen."

"But now that Ursula has returned…" I didn't need to finish the question. It was clear who was behind her attack, and it wasn't much of a stretch to think she might be responsible for Morgan, too. From the look on Dante's face, I imagined he was wondering the same thing.

"You see why she needs you?" His hand found mine again, and he squeezed it desperately. "Why *I* need you?"

My stomach knotted at the thought of spending more time with Ursula. It was only made worse when I contemplated how she'd react if she found out that Raphael was dead and that I was more or less to blame.

"You have dozens of guards." I gave Dante a pleading frown and waited to see if he would threaten Roman's life. Or Mandy's. This nice act of his was hard to swallow. I didn't trust it.

"None of my guards have the Eye of Blood," he said. "And none know the truth of this delicate matter—nor can they. It would compromise your safety, and as cruel as you may think I am, I do not wish to see harm come to you."

I wanted to believe him, but the nervous hum twisting its way through my body wasn't for fear of Dante alone. "Does Kassandra know I saved the queen?"

"Everyone knows, my dear." His brows drew up in surprise. "Why do you think you are here and not locked in a coffin after your slight against House Sorano?"

"Oh…" I was an idiot. An ignorant, ungrateful child was not far off the mark at all.

"You have been quite lucky for an impulsive vampling," Dante said. A tired smile creased his face. "I hope you will lend me and my cousin—*our* cousin—some of that luck."

"Do I have a choice?"

"There is always a choice." He released my hand and picked up the teapot, pouring us each a third helping of blood. "Though, I very much suspect that the court will issue a formal summons for your presence if you do not attend."

"What? Why?"

"Because you were crucial in Ursula's…return," he said. "If you are not there to support her, they will assume they can use you to prove her guilt."

I took the cup he offered with a frown. "You're not asking me to lie under oath, are you?"

"Of course not. But I would be remiss if I didn't advocate for extra care and compassion if you are asked to recount the details of that night. Be gentle with Ursula. I know twenty years seems like an awfully long time, but she and Morgan shared a bond that does not come close to any I have seen before, and grief makes sad fools of the best of us."

His remark brought my mother to mind. I knew a thing or two about grieving and the struggle that was letting go and moving on. Maybe if I tried to see that in Ursula, I could stand to be around her for more than five minutes without wanting to strangle her.

Sure, she'd sired a couple of homicidal heathens. My mother had given birth to Laura. No one was perfect.

Dante's hand touched mine again, and I jumped.

"Help me protect Ursula from Kassandra and the vultures on the council," he said. "And I shall do everything in my power to convince your future sire that your calling is with Blood Vice."

"And you'll take the truth about my sire to your grave," I added. If we were striking a bargain, I'd settle for nothing short of his word not to blackmail me.

"You have my word," he said, eyes locking with mine. My heart flipflopped hesitantly.

"And I want my guns back."

"I will make sure you have them before the hearing."

"Magazines fully loaded."

His mouth twitched up in a small grin. "Does this mean we have an accord?"

How could we not at this point? He was agreeing to my every demand—though a little too easily. It felt like a trap. But it was a trap in which I'd be armed and allowed to leave the manor.

"We have a deal."

Chapter Seven

I couldn't shake the buzz in my veins after the meeting with Dante. Of course, spilling my guts and gambling away my future was only half responsible for that. I'd had an awful lot of blood tonight. Rich blood, too.

I paced my room, hoping to dispel some of the nervous energy before sunrise. The mess in Ursula's room had been cleaned up, and she was back where she belonged and out of my hair. *For now.*

There were a half-dozen guards out on the terrace and more in the hallway, so I wouldn't be expected to do any actual bodyguarding until we left for the trial Friday evening. I was pretty sure my presence would be mostly for show anyway, considering how Dante had used my name to keep Ursula from being whisked off to someplace unknown.

Tuesday night had bled into Wednesday morning, and now it felt as if everything were happening too fast. I hated the way time worked for vampires, every night swallowing up two dates, making them seem too long and too short at the same time.

I changed out of my black sweater and tights and into yoga pants and a long-sleeved tee shirt, opting for a green one rather than the black I'd been favoring of late. If Ursula decided to drop in on me uninvited again, she was going to have to work harder for her insults.

I paced some more, wishing Mandy were around to talk to—now that I actually had something worth talking about. I hoped she was enjoying working with the Cadaver Dogs, though, and that she was being safe.

Roman crossed my mind next, and I prayed for his safety, too. His silence wounded me, but the yearning I still felt for him suggested that our bond wasn't as broken as he'd tried to convince me it was. Either that or I was afflicted with something more pathetic and mundane than I cared to admit.

Unrequited love. *Ick*.

By the time the sky lit up with the first hints of sunrise, I was ready for it. I lay back on my bed, welcoming the reprieve from reality. Welcoming the temporary death that visited me each morning and slipped out with the sun every night.

I rose Wednesday night feeling no better off.

My room had been cleaned while I slept. The scent of lavender and lemon filled the air, and the wooden furnishings shined with fresh wax. The closet door stood open, and on the inside hook hung a garment bag with a note. I slid off the bed and crossed the room to read it.

Guard wardrobe for trial — Jenna Skye.

I fingered open the fold of the bag and peeked inside, finding a deep red cloak and a stretchy, black bodysuit. What the hell kind of nonsense was this? If Little Red had joined a guild of assassins, maybe it wouldn't be so out of place in her closet. But for a trial? What was Dante thinking?

I abandoned the fashion nightmare and found a heavy paper shopping bag propped against the dresser. A painter's palette logo was stamped on the front, and inside, I found a spiral-ring sketchpad and several boxes of high-end drawing pencils and charcoals.

Recreating Raphael's portrait wasn't something I was looking forward to. It wouldn't be a physically challenging task, but the thought of bringing his hateful face to life on the page again bothered me. I didn't need the reminder of the scars he'd left on me and those I loved.

I emptied the bag of art supplies onto my bed and soon found myself sketching a portrait of Will instead. Charcoal and pastels stained my fingers as I smudged out the shadows along his hairline and under the apples of his cheeks. I added more lines at the corners of his eyes, enhancing his smile. It wasn't my best work—I was out of practice—but when I finished, the likeness was close enough that it tugged at my heartstrings.

Maybe I could agree with Ursula on one thing. Gifts were best not wasted on undeserving subjects.

I drew a few more practice portraits. Mandy and Serena huddled together, eating popcorn on the couch. Laura and her ridiculous Chihuahua, Duncan, surrounded by a heap of her designer luggage. Roman, hair mussed and lids half-parted over his icy blues, elbows propped on the pillows behind him.

By then, I was fully warmed up. And thirsty.

I didn't bother changing before I slipped out of my room and headed for the harem. The hallway was lined with guards, and though they watched me with skeptical reserve, no one tried to stop me or asked what I thought I was doing. I passed Murphy on my way upstairs.

"Evening," he said with a nod, then touched a finger to the side of his nose. "Looks like you found the goodies the boss sent Yosh to fetch for ya."

"Oh, hell." I reached for my face, stopping short of it when I noticed my blackened fingertips. "Guess I should have cleaned up first."

"There's a washroom on the harem level," he said. "Last door on the right before you reach the kitchen."

"Thanks."

He called over his shoulder as I continued up the stairs. "The boss says you're coming with us Friday—as a guard." I couldn't decide if he sounded dismayed or merely confused.

"Looks like it."

"Gym's on the main level of the north wing," he said. "I'll be in there after my shift ends around four-thirty. You know, in case you'd like someone to spar with. Gotta stay sharp."

"Right. Yeah, sure." I pointed a finger at him before noticing once again how filthy I was.

"Catch you later." Murphy gave me another nod and then headed down the stairs with extra bounce in his step.

His enthusiasm made me wonder if working out with the duke's guards was such a good idea. I was a vampling, and any accomplishment, no matter how slight, seemed to make everyone eager to reestablish the pecking order.

I considered all the ways I might regret my decision to join Murphy in the gym as I scrubbed the charcoal from my hands and face in the washroom upstairs. When I made it to the harem kitchen, I was surprised to find a much larger crowd than I'd seen the night before.

Every barstool at the counter was occupied, and most of the chairs and sofas in the lounge were, too. At least thirty humans chattered over the televisions and each other. Some snacked on fruit and nuts, and others ate from bowls of salad or stew. A few looked up as I stopped at the counter, and I wondered if I'd come at a bad time.

"Jenna!" Yoshiko waved to me from the other side of the kitchen where she stood in front of the stove stirring several stock pots. She slipped off the apron she wore and handed it to another woman as I circled to her side of the counter, excusing myself as I squeezed past a pair of donors.

"I didn't mean to interrupt your dinner."

She shook her head. "I've already eaten, and everyone here knows how to help themselves," she said, shooting a snarky grin at a man refilling his bowl at the stove. "Would you like a blood pot? We have a few donors available right now."

"A pot would be great." I gave her an apologetic smile. Drinking from a donor would have been easier and not created more dirty dishes—which it looked as if there would be plenty of once dinnertime was over—but I just couldn't. Maybe I'd reconsider after the trial.

"One blood pot, coming right up." Yoshiko found a tray and loaded it with everything she'd need before heading down the back hallway. I watched her go, taking in the doors spaced on either side. It reminded me of the harem at the bat cave, only with less concrete.

While I waited for Yoshiko to return, more donors took notice of me. Their curious glances and timid smiles were unsettling. It was like being back at Bleeders, except there was no skull-pounding music or flashing lights or other vampires to dilute the attention. And I was woefully underdressed.

When Yoshiko came back with my blood pot, I couldn't get out of there fast enough. I retreated to my room to drink in peace, and then set to work drawing my murderer.

There was an extra level of discomfort while drawing Raphael this time. I nestled in against my headboard and pulled the sketchpad up onto my folded knees. My hands shook, and my eyes kept darting to the bedroom door. I had a horrible vision of Ursula barging in uninvited. She'd take one look at her scion's likeness, and all hell would break loose.

It occurred to me, halfway through the drawing, that I didn't know what Raphael looked like when he wasn't snapping and snarling, fangs fully extended and eyes wild with euphoric violence. He couldn't have looked like that all the time, though that was how he appeared whenever he emerged from the shadows of my psyche.

I finished the rendering in a hurry and then closed the sketchpad before stuffing it under the mattress of my bed. I wasn't sure what else to do with it until I saw the duke again, but I certainly couldn't leave it lying around for anyone to find.

Paranoia was not a good substitute for boredom, and the night was still young. The span of time from sundown to sunup had just dipped below the fourteen-hour mark, half an hour less than it had been at Midwinter, and would steadily decline until reaching just over nine hours at Midsummer. When the queen would announce my adoptive sire.

With nothing much to do with myself until then, it seemed like an eternity away. My deal with Dante to attend Ursula's trial suddenly felt like a favor he was doing for me instead of the other way around. I needed out of this room—

out of this house.

My eyes closed, and I tried to envision what Mandy might be doing right this moment. Maybe running through the woods, the waxing moon's light flickering through naked branches. Cold air straining her lungs. Some tender prey— anything but a house cat—just ahead.

I wished I was out there with her.

When I couldn't take it any longer, I slipped from my room again and made my way to the library. Ursula and I were nowhere near friends, but I was less fearful of her since our last encounter. I skimmed Dante's collection for familiar titles I'd read at the bat cave. Then I found a copy of *The Blood Will Run* in the poetry section and settled into an overstuffed armchair to read it. I'd been too desperate for hard information to enjoy leisure reads during training.

Time slipped by more easily, and the next time I glanced up at the clock, it was creeping past four in the morning. I tucked the book of vampiric poems back in place on its shelf and left, heading for the north stairwell.

The gym in the duke's manor was located directly beneath the library. There was an elevated sparring ring off to left side of the room, and some free weights and equipment scattered throughout the rest of the space. A few punching bags hung from the ceiling, and a rotating, rock-climbing wall filled the northwest corner.

That's where I found Murphy, doing one-handed pullups from a protruding nub of faux rock. *Shirtless*. I hadn't realized just how stacked he was, hidden beneath the black suit uniform all the guards wore. His muscles glistened as if they'd been rubbed down with oil—or as if he'd been in here a while warming up.

"There you are," he said, beaming at me as he dropped down from the rock wall.

"I'm ten minutes early." I pointed at the clock above the door. "How long have you been at it?"

"Not long." Murphy grabbed a towel draped over the back of a leg press machine and wiped his face with it.

"Do you always get lubed up before working out?"

"What? No." He blushed and looked at his chest before moving the towel down to scrub away the evidence.

Voices filtered into the room as the door opened and five more guards joined us. Their eyes landed on me, and smug grins spread across their faces. Their complete lack of surprise was not a good sign. That Murphy didn't seem surprised was worse.

I folded my arms. "I take it you're not wanting to lift weights or run on the treadmills?"

"Where's the fun in that?" Murphy asked.

"I'm not interested in a pissing match. I thought you were one of the nice guys."

"I am," he insisted. "Come on, now. It's not like that. Just a little friendly competition. You're going to be working with us this weekend. We want to see what you've got."

One of the newcomers slapped him on the back. "Murphy here won the privilege of challenging you since he out lifted us all last night."

"And ain't a friendlier face around here than his," another teased.

If I were going to spar with anyone, I supposed Murphy would have been my top pick—even if he did make Wolverine look like an eighties aerobics instructor. Still, full disclosure would have been nice. No one liked being ganged up on.

"His face might not look so friendly once I'm done with it," I said. Murphy smirked, and one of the guards shook his shoulders with gleeful anticipation.

We made our way to the ring, and someone tossed me a pair of blue sparring gloves. The sessions at the bat cave were done bare-knuckled, but I didn't complain. The gloves would soften my blows, but they would also take the edge off Murphy's hits that were no doubt heavier than mine.

"Don't worry," he said, tightening his laces. "I'll take it easy on you."

"Where's the fun in that?" I snapped back.

His sincerity grated on me. I could tell that the rest of the guards thought he was teasing, but I heard his words for what they were. They all wanted to knock me down a peg. Murphy had fought for the honor to make sure things didn't get out of hand, which only made me want to prove myself more.

I was a vampling. Not an invalid.

"Ding ding!" one of the guards called out jokingly, launching our match.

The sparring ring platform bounced softly beneath my feet as Murphy sprang into action, playfully jabbing the air in front of him. This was all a big joke, and everyone expected me to be the punchline. The saddest part was that I welcomed the distraction.

Murphy moved forward and threw a few light hooks that I easily dodged or parried without giving him too much ground. On his last swing, I slipped in and delivered a sharp uppercut to his ribcage.

"Ooh, good one," he said, a wince tightening his smile. "Thought you were a southpaw."

"What would give you that idea?" I asked, deliberately not confirming his suspicion.

"You had more charcoal on your left hand when I caught you on your way up to the harem."

"Been sizing me up all night, huh?"

Murphy grinned and threw another wide hook, but this time, he kept his left elbow tucked in close to his side. I blocked his punch with the back of my left hand and planted a nasty jab straight to his nose with my right. He bled instantly, his head reeling from the force of the hit.

The guards *oohed* and *aahed* at the exchange as the humor in the room grew tense. Their laughter had a nervous edge to it, and their chants of encouragement were less certain than before.

Murphy wiped the back of one glove under his nose and glanced down at the blood that came away. His eyes narrowed on me, and I guessed that we were done playing footsie.

The next jab he threw my way was followed by a hook that grazed my temple and sent me back a step. He moved in fast, forcing me closer to the ropes at my back. I pivoted out of the corner and let him dance me to the opposite side of the ring, buying all the space I could with short jabs until I took a chance and aimed a knee up at his ribs.

Murphy had been waiting for it. He hooked his arm under my leg while his shoulder simultaneously rammed into my stomach. I flopped against his slick back and was suddenly wrenched off my feet. As I slipped toward the floor where he intended to body slam me, rather than brace for the impact, I looped an arm around Murphy's neck and jerked hard.

The move wasn't the smartest, seeing as how he landed on top of me after my head hit the floor, but I hung on when he tried to get up, locking both arms together in a chokehold that yielded a satisfying gagging sound from him.

My leg was still hooked over the bend of his elbow, so I tucked my foot behind his hip, pinning his arm back as he tried to sit up. Murphy's free hand connected with my face behind his head, but the angle wasn't ideal. It didn't tickle, but it wasn't painful enough for me to give up the leverage. I lost a little of that resolve when he threw his body back and slammed me to the floor again.

"Come on, Murph!" a guard shouted. "You're getting your ass handed to you by a girl!"

"Yeah, Murphster." I grunted in his ear as I struggled to keep my arms locked around his neck. "What is this? A bake-off?"

"No," he growled. "It's your funeral."

The insult more than his next body slam knocked the air from my lungs. He probably hadn't meant anything cruel by it, but the reminder sent a wave of boiling rage through my veins, and my hold on him tightened as my fangs slipped free with a furious hiss.

"H-hey," he stammered through clenched teeth. "No fangs!"

"Dare I ask what is going on here?"

We glanced up to find Dante peering at us through the sparring ring ropes. His eyes fixed on Murphy first but zeroed in on me next as we released each other and collapsed to the ring floor.

"Are you all right, Ms. Skye?" Dante asked.

"I almost had him," I gasped as I rolled onto my stomach and pushed myself up.

Murphy made a sound that crossed between a snort and a wheeze. "In your dreams."

Dante frowned at him. "You better put some ice on that nose. The queen will not be pleased if my personal guards are not presentable."

"Yes, Your Grace." Murphy bowed his head, and the rest of the guards followed suit as the duke glanced their way.

Dante turned back to me again. "If you are done, Ms. Skye, I would like to go over a few things with you regarding this weekend."

"I'm done—for now," I said, shooting Murphy a sharp grin—though not as sharp as before the duke had arrived. I was a little embarrassed that my fangs had popped free in the heat of the moment, but my blood vision had stayed under control, so there was that.

I peeled off the sparring gloves and tossed them to one of the guards before leaving the gym with Dante. His scrutiny as we walked down the hall toward the foyer made me blush. I wiped my sweaty hands down the front of my yoga pants and readjusted my ponytail.

"Are you sure you are all right?" he asked again.

"I survived training at the BATC. I think I can handle a little sparring with one of your guards."

"One of my *best* guards." A concerned frown creased his forehead. "Who seemed to be rather fond of you, so I am not sure how you ended up at such odds."

I shook my head. "We were just messing around."

"Hmmm." He blinked and glanced away from me to acknowledge the guards stationed outside his office doors as we passed through the foyer. It was just a subtle dip of his head to each of them. A silent *thank you for your service.*

"If Murphy is one of your best guards, why didn't you take him with you on your disrupted Denver trip?" I asked after we'd entered the south wing hallway.

"Because Ursula needed his protection more than I did."

"Good call."

He sighed and folded his hands behind his back. "Not good enough, apparently."

"That's not Murphy's fault."

"Of course not," he said. "He cannot be everywhere at once, and I am sure even if the assassin had not made it past the perimeter, the council would have used it to their advantage."

We neared my room, and I noticed a guard standing just outside the door, holding two pistol cases.

"Is that... Are those..." My breath hitched hopefully,

and Dante's nervous grimace was all the confirmation I needed.

"Thank you," he said, taking the cases from the guard. "I shall be fine," he added as the man made to follow us inside my bedroom. "You may return to your scheduled post."

The guard shot me a nervous glance but bowed his head obediently. "Your Grace."

"Come." Dante nodded me farther into the room and closed the door behind us with his elbow. "I do not have much time to spare."

"Is my Browning in one of those?" The gun had belonged to my mother, and the last time I'd seen it was when Vanessa confiscated it from me in the field behind Ursula's safehouse. She'd also taken my mother's old Mossberg shotgun.

"Do you have a drawing for me?" Dante asked, laying one of the cases down on the gray duvet cover. I huffed and circled the bed to dig out the sketchpad from under my mattress. He crept closer, but I turned my back to keep the other drawings from his view as I flipped to the portrait of Raphael.

"There." I turned around and held it up to him. "Happy?"

He took the pad from me and cringed. "It is hard to be certain with his face in such...*pandemonium*."

I stared at him long and hard. "He was *killing* me—and not with kindness."

"Point taken."

"So…my guns." I pointed a finger at the case he'd left on my bed. "May I?"

Dante nodded, and I eagerly popped open the laches. My range Glock and the .380 Mandy had salvaged from my kitchen were nestled down inside foam cutouts on either side of my mother's Browning. Bittersweet relief squeezed my heart as I ran my fingertips over the vintage pistol's barrel.

"I left your shotgun in storage," Dante said. "You will not be needing it this weekend—and I would really prefer that you use the Reaper TDs the rest of the royal guards carry."

He dropped the second case on the bed beside the first and opened the lid, revealing a pair of .40 calibers tucked in foam cutouts that were better fitting than those around my personal firearms. I picked one up and tested its weight. The grip texture felt nice against my hand.

"Reaper TD?" I echoed.

"True Death," he explained. "They are a specialty model."

"Sorano Munitions?"

"And the guard uniform holsters are designed for them."

"Uniform? You mean the catsuit and the Renaissance fair cape?" I snorted and put the gun back in the case, taking note of the series of empty cutouts in the foam beneath the firearms. When I turned back to Dante, I found him fingering through my earlier drawings. My face burned as he paused on the one of Roman and cocked an eyebrow at me.

"The guard uniforms are made from material akin to shark-resistant wetsuits," he said as he closed the sketchpad and handed it back to me. I snatched it from him with a scowl. "And the cloaks are made from the same material as bomb blankets. They are quite expensive, and you should be honored to have one."

"I'm…overjoyed," I said dryly, biting off the word as I snapped the gun cases shut. "But I'd be even more thrilled if these guns were loaded and I had the extra magazines I'm sure come standard with them."

"Friday night, before we leave." Dante gave me an apologetic smile. "Humor me for one more night. Give my advisors extra time to warm to the idea."

"Uh-huh."

"And perhaps work on your etiquette," he added. "It will be expected of you in the formal presence of the council and the crown. The royal family does not take kindly to disrespectful subjects."

"Yes, Your Grace." I dipped into an exaggerated bow, but he quickly pulled me upright by my chin, drawing a gasp from me. His chestnut-colored eyes searched mine.

"Do not make me regret this, Ms. Skye."

Chapter Eight

Mandy returned before sunset Thursday night. I woke with her arms wrapped around my waist and her head nuzzled against my stomach. She smelled like pizza and car air freshener, so I knew she couldn't have been back for long. Her hair stirred in the wind of my reanimated breath, rousing her instantly.

"Yoshiko told me about the assassin," she said, crushing me in a bear hug. "If I'd been here, I would have eaten his face clean off."

"Uh, thanks." I wriggled away from her and tried to sit up. "How was working with the Cadaver Dogs? Did you help them crack a tough case?"

"We tracked down the daughter of the Álvarez Pack's alpha. She'd been buried alive—even though the ransom was paid." Mandy didn't sound as thrilled as I expected her to be over such an accomplishment.

"Did she…survive?"

"Yeah." Mandy chewed her bottom lip, and her eyebrows knit together as she tucked a lock of unruly hair behind her ear. "We even found the creeps who abducted her, but someone beat us to them, and they took the money, too."

"The girl's dad?"

Mandy shook her head. "I don't think so. He wouldn't

have had the opportunity—he was with the search party the whole time."

"Huh." I shrugged. "Well, at least you saved the girl."

"One of them." She pressed her lips together, but her chin trembled anyway. "Serena dumped me."

"Oh, sweetie." I opened my arms, inviting her to abuse my ribs some more. "I'm so sorry."

"She said she needed someone who could be there for her, and that I hadn't been lately." Mandy sobbed against my shoulder, taking deep, gasping breaths as I stroked her back.

"Maybe she just needs some time," I suggested. "After everything that's happened—"

"No. She hates me, and she has every right to." Mandy sniffled and pulled away from me.

"She doesn't hate you."

"She should. I've been keeping the truth from her. About you and her dad. About *me*. It's just too much. You know? Living with all this guilt all the time. It's better this way. She'll find someone who deserves her. Someone who isn't a monster—"

"You're *not* a monster." I squeezed her shoulders.

"I am," she insisted. "I have to be. Especially this weekend."

"You're coming to the trial?"

"I'm your official daylight attendant, sworn to watch over

you while you rest." The pride in her voice fell flat. "I'll be sharing a suite with the duchess's harem when off-duty, but you get to bunk with ol' Red herself." Like I needed anything else to look forward to.

"Maybe the trial won't carry into a second night?" I gave Mandy a strained smile.

"Yeah, and maybe you'll stop oversharing with our benevolent jailer." She leaned over the edge of the bed and stuffed her hand between the mattresses, coming away with my sketchpad. "I saw who you drew in here, and I can smell the duke on it."

"It's not what you think." I held up my hands, and she huffed at my embarrassed surprise.

"I swear, I'm gone for two nights. *Two* nights."

"There was no way around it, and at least now he knows about Kassandra, and I obviously didn't tell him *how* Raphael kicked off," I hissed under my breath. "I mean, I didn't actually *see* how it happened, so…what was there to tell? What's the harm in assuming he burned up in the sun? And besides, the duke is in no hurry to share the news with the world."

Mandy's nostrils flared. "Blabberfangs."

"Really? You're gonna resort to name-calling?"

"Don't you know that loose lips sink ships?"

"Good thing we're not pirates then." I folded my arms

and copied her indignant scowl.

"Yeah, well, snitches get stitches," she tried again.

"If you lie down with dogs, you get up with fleas."

"Where?" she squealed, grabbing a handful of her hair. "Did you see one?"

I snorted out a laugh before I could stop myself, and Mandy smacked me across the face with a pillow, knocking me off the bed. I curled into a ball on the floor, still cackling as she straddled my legs and attempted to smother me with the pillow.

"I didn't mean it," I said in between laughs, gasping for air.

"Say you're sorry!" she demanded.

"I'm sorry! I'm sorry!"

"You don't sound sorry. You sound like an asshole."

"I'm an asshole, and I'm sorry."

I couldn't stop laughing, and soon, Mandy was laughing, too. It felt good. And needed.

"I missed you," she admitted once we calmed down and caught our breaths. I grinned and let her help me off the floor.

"I missed you, too."

"Oh!" Her face lit up, and she bounced on her toes. "Wait till you see the fancy costumes we get to wear this weekend."

Chapter Nine

The night passed too quickly with Mandy's return and the impending trial. We visited the library and the gym, though I didn't see Murphy. I suspected he'd been given some time off to rest up for the weekend venture.

Mandy and I dropped by the harem, too. I was surprised to see how well she was getting on with the house donors. She pointed out a few that I hadn't realized were werewolves, and they spoke about who all would be coming with us for the trial and who would be staying behind. Some sounded a bit jealous to be missing out on such a high-profile event, while others seemed relieved.

Sooner than I would have liked, it was Friday evening, and we were preparing to leave the manor.

"I can't stop touching myself," Mandy said as she gazed into the mirror on the inside of my closet door. Her hands smoothed over her stomach and breasts, caressing the skintight guard uniform. "Does this thing make me look like a porn star?" She glanced over her shoulder and caught sight of me in my own catsuit. "Because it *definitely* makes you look like a porn star."

"What? No." I nudged her aside to look at myself in the mirror. "Okay, maybe a little," I admitted.

"Uh-huh." Mandy turned around to get a peek at her butt

in the mirror's reflection. "Oh, yeah. Total slutsville."

"Maybe the cloaks of elvenkind will tone it down a bit," I grumbled.

Someone pounded on the bedroom door, and I attempted to cover myself despite being fully concealed from the neck down. I snatched up the red wrap from my bed and threw it over my shoulders.

"Special delivery," Murphy called from out in the hall.

"Just a minute!"

Mandy snickered and leaned against the closet door, watching me fumble with the drawstring at my throat. She didn't seem bothered by how little the uniform left to the imagination, but then again, she was comfortable licking her own butt in wolf form so she couldn't be expected to adhere to the standard principals of modesty.

I finally gave up and held the mantle closed with one hand as I crossed the room and opened the door for Murphy. He filled the doorway, clad in his own leathery one-piece, red cloak spilling behind his shoulders. An ammo box was tucked under one arm. The handle of a gun case that matched the one Dante had delivered the pair of Reaper TDs in was grasped in his opposite hand.

"Hello, mooseknuckle," Mandy said under her breath as Murphy joined us in the room. He blinked at her, taking in her uniform with dispassionate eyes.

"Boss was right," he finally said. "You're far too skinny for the .40s. Stiff breeze, and they'll knock you right over."

She glanced down at his crotch. "Stiff breeze and you might become an innie."

"Ooh, big bad wolf. Why don't you do some huffing and puffing and find out?"

"Is this the one you wiped the gym floor with?" Mandy asked, hiking a thumb at him. Murphy's head jerked back, and he gaped at me.

"That was a draw! We were interrupted," he balked. "I want a rematch."

I pressed my lips together, trying to hide my amusement at his outrage. "Sure. After the trial."

His brow and chin crumpled as he dropped the gun case on my bed and shot Mandy an unfriendly look. "I brought you new toys, too."

"I'd rather shift than use a gun any day," she said, though her eyes lingered on the case as he set the ammo box down beside it.

"These are the Reaper TD 9Cs." Murphy opened the case and twisted it around so Mandy could get a better look at them. "They're a lot like the .40s, just a compacted 9mm variety." There were six additional magazines tucked in the foam beneath the pistols. He opened the ammo box and unpacked eight larger magazines, handing them to me.

"The duke said something about holsters?" I said, clutching the cloak tighter around my neck.

Murphy gave me a tight grin. "Ditch the outerwear. You don't have anything I ain't seen before, and it's going to be hard showing you all your suit's hiding places with that thing in the way."

I groaned and rolled my eyes, but I did as he said, discarding the cloak and throwing it down on the bed. Murphy cleared his throat and cocked his head at my Reaper TD gun case. I'd stashed the one with my personal firearms in the back of the closet, having nowhere better to keep them.

The TDs had a solid feel to them. Their grips were thicker than I would have preferred, but they were shaped and textured in such a way that I didn't think I'd have any problems handling them. I ejected their empty magazines and traded them out with a pair of the loaded ones Murphy had brought before turning around to catch him gawking at my ass.

"I will kill you dead." With the two pistols in my hands, the threat ripped his eyes away instantly.

"Panels!" He shook his head and slapped his ribcage on either side. "Right beside your—under your arms," he said, easing a step away from me.

I felt along the odd folds of the material, occasionally glancing up to make sure he wasn't ogling. Just as my finger hooked inside a mesh-lined pouch and I began to see how a gun barrel might fit in there, Mandy clicked her tongue.

"Done," she announced, patting the pair of 9mm nestled under her arms. "Now, where do the magazines go?" She ran her hands down the insides of her thighs and then over her hips, shamelessly searching for more pockets as she felt herself up.

Murphy turned to instruct her by pointing out the subtle bulges on his uniform that encircled his waist like a belt. I took the opportunity to slide my pistols in place without an audience and then began tucking away my own magazines. With my blond braid, I looked like Assassin Barbie. My decorum and the red cloak called to me from where I'd abandoned them on the bed.

Once we were all loaded up with artillery and overnight bags—and fully dressed—Murphy led us to the garage located at the end of the north wing. Lights glared down from the cavernous ceiling, reflecting off a brigade of shiny, black vehicles parked two deep and three wide. I spotted a large SUV parked against the far wall. It reminded me of the ones used by Blood Vice, complete with puck antennas spaced out in a line across the roof. The rest of the vehicles were larger sedans, all spotless and perfectly aligned, facing the closed overhead door.

A guard slipped in behind us and patted Murphy on the

shoulder before moving out of the way for a pair of harem donors. Before long, we were joined by enough people in hooded cloaks to perform a Satanic ritual.

"Just for the record, I'm not a virgin," Mandy announced. "You know, in case the evening agenda involves any sacrifices."

"Really?" Murphy gasped. "You're not? How shocking."

"Stuff it, mooseknuckle."

He snickered, but then his face grew serious as he clapped his hands to garner everyone's attention.

"The duke and duchess will be with us in a moment, so let's get situated," he said, glancing over the gathered crowd. "Who here is with the harem?"

Five humans and one of the wolves Mandy had introduced me to lifted their hands into the air. "Six. That's everyone." Murphy nodded at one of the vampy guards. "Y'all will be riding with Lane in the SUV. Go ahead and get loaded up," he said, passing off Mandy's and my overnight bags to one of the donors. Apparently, they were in charge of luggage, too.

We were left with a guard I recognized from the gym, one I'd never noticed before, and the two wolves Mandy lovingly referred to as Tweedledee and Tweedledum. They seemed less annoyed to see her, which made me wonder if she'd earned some sliver of their respect while they were out hunting down the wolfy princess together.

"Skye and Starsgard will ride in my car with the duke and duchess," Murphy said. "The rest of you go with Donnie, who'll take lead. I'll follow, and Lane will play caboose with the harem wagon."

"Yes, sir," the men echoed and then headed off to one of the shiny black cars just as Belinda delivered the royal fam to the garage's north wing entrance.

The duke and duchess wore the same red cloaks as everyone else, but the similarity stopped there. Dante had slicked his hair back again, and he wore a collared dress shirt with a red, baroque waistcoat and black trousers. If he popped out his fangs, he would have been ready for a Halloween contest.

Ursula was less obvious in a lacey, gray sheath dress, though the blood-red cloak transformed every ensemble, making the wearer appear as if they might be on a quest to Mount Doom. It wasn't really a garment that could be dressed up or down.

I was more surprised to find Belinda without a cloak. She lingered in the doorway in a flared skirt and cardigan and waved to Murphy and me.

"Check in once you're settled," she said before offering Dante and Ursula a farewell bow. "Be safe, Your Graces." Then she disappeared inside the manor, closing the door behind her.

The duke turned to take in my *uniform* with an appreciative once-over. "It suits you."

My cheeks warmed, but I bit my tongue, refraining from threatening him the way I had Murphy. Compared to what I was used to wearing on the human police force—and even with Blood Vice—the royal guard uniform felt entirely undignified and ridiculous.

"Shouldn't we be on our way?" Ursula asked, shooting Dante a dirty look. "I'm ready to get this over with. Coffin-lock or royal tongue-lashing, either one is better than staying holed up here forever."

"Such a gracious guest you are, cousin." Dante sighed and held his hand out to her, but she shooed it away and whisked past him toward one of the sedans. Murphy trotted to catch up, passing her in time to open the back door.

This was going to be loads of fun. I could already tell.

Mandy called dibs on the front passenger seat of the sedan. Murphy was driving, so that left me sandwiched in the back seat between the duke and duchess. It was roomy, but not nearly spacious enough for all the family drama that filled the air with awkward tension.

"How far away is the venue?" I asked.

"Twenty minutes." Dante gazed out his window at the city lights that glowed against the sky in the distance. We were heading east, toward downtown St. Louis. I caught a glimpse of the Gateway Arch through the buildings as we neared it.

"Tell me something I don't know about this trial," I begged Dante, desperate for a break in the silence.

Ursula scoffed. "It's a steaming shit pile of lies designed to dismantle the royal family."

"The lords and ladies who rule over the elite vampire families in this country each hold a single seat on the Vampiric High Council," Dante said, ignoring Ursula's vulgar outburst. "But only seven are called upon to determine the outcome of any given trial. There is a regional drawing process so that the selection is diverse and balanced."

"Because at least half of them are malicious, power-hungry vultures," Ursula injected.

"The seven councilors are not announced beforehand in an effort to prevent blackmail threats and bribes," Dante went on. "Only the committee who issues the summons is aware of who they are before the trial begins."

The duke's willingness to share information was refreshing. It had been such an effort with Roman, as if he had struggled to attain the knowledge himself and thought I should have to endure the same. I imagined it was harder for him as a human—and with someone like Vanessa for a potential sire, who'd had patience hammered into her as a core virtue by the likes of Faye Sorano.

I wasn't asking for damning secrets—I just wanted enough detail to gain a bearing on the situation. Half the time, Dante offered that without even having to be asked. He went over all the trial specifics he was aware of on the drive across the city, occasionally pausing to answer my sidebar questions while Ursula rolled her eyes.

The hearing was being held at the Nightfall Opera House, owned by none other than Radu Vlad, the owner of Bleeders. The in-house suites that usually accommodated the ballet troupes and actors who traveled far and wide to perform at the theater had been offered to the royal family and the council members who were chosen to pass judgment on Ursula.

The duke's mellow voice calmed my nerves. His tenor encompassed Bob Ross and Morgan Freeman with a touch of Enrique Iglesias. I imagined that voice reading the erotic poems I'd found in the manor library and had to remind myself that I hated this guy and his murderous, bloodsucking family that had stolen my mortality.

When our small procession slowed near a quieter slice of downtown and entered a parking garage, an electric hum took up residence in my veins once again.

Murphy followed the lead car up to the second level and backed us into a parking slot angled against an internal wall, while the harem SUV pulled in sideways and blocked off the four adjacent spaces. As we exited the vehicles and regrouped, six newcomers in white robes approached us. They bowed to the duke but made a point to ignore the duchess.

"We're under council orders to escort the duchess to the defendant chamber until the hearing begins," one of them announced.

Ursula bristled, but Dante touched her shoulder before she could protest. "Of course. But given the recent attack, you will understand if I send two of my personal guards to ensure her safety."

The mouthpiece for the white cloaks didn't look pleased about having their competence challenged, but he bowed stiffly at the duke. "Yes, Your Grace."

Dante nodded to Murphy and Donnie, and the two vampires fell into place at Ursula's sides, creating a buffer that dissuaded the council wardens from touching the duchess. It was enough to compel her cooperation, though she shot Dante a pleading scowl as they led her away.

"We shall see you soon, cousin," he called after her.

Lane, the remaining vampiric guard, took up a post on the opposite side of the duke from me, while Mandy took her place with the werewolves flanking the blood donors. Only vampires were allowed to attend the actual trial, so I assumed the remaining guard who had come with us was half-sired. He stayed close to the harem.

Together, our merry lot marched down the descending drive and exited onto the sidewalk. More vehicles approached and entered the garage farther down. I watched them carefully, taking note of the out-of-state plates as we crossed the street.

The Nightfall Opera House's mottled gray brickwork and arched windows wouldn't have seemed out of place tucked among the cathedrals and museums of Vatican City. Torches lit with actual fire lined the stairs leading up to three sets of double doors. It was the perfect place for a medieval dinner theater—or for a vampiric inquisition.

More white cloaks met us in the lobby, but they were friendlier than Ursula's greeting party had been. And human, Mandy informed me in a rushed whisper as the harem party diverged and was led away to a reserved suite upstairs. They would be served a meal and offered entertainment until the trial recessed for daybreak.

Inside the theater hall, the stage had been set for the hearing. Seven high-backed chairs with leather upholstery were grouped together to the right, three staggered in front of the other four. To the left, another leather seat had been enclosed by a short, paneled wall similar to a witness stand in a courtroom. And in the very center of the stage sat an unembellished wooden chair. It was so glaringly obvious that I was almost surprised a dunce cap hadn't been hooked over one of the back posts.

Beyond the curtains that framed the stage, golden walls curved up and out. A pale-yellow ivy pattern created subtle texture and was repeated in the intricate trim outlining a dozen balconies that spanned the theater walls.

Another white cloak directed the duke through an arched opening. Lane and I followed, climbing a winding staircase that opened to the curtained alcoves backing the balconies. Our usher left us at the mouth of one before disappearing down the stairs as more guests arrived.

I parted the curtains and examined the balcony, taking in the velvet chairs and the gold railing. For good measure, I ran my hand under the seats, checking for any mysterious devices—like bugs or bombs.

"Keep watch for my sister and the prince," Dante said to Lane. "Inform me as soon as they arrive." It took me a moment to realize he was talking about Kassandra. His *sister*. That was a scary thought.

Lane nodded and gave us his back, training his gaze on the stairwell. The traffic inside the theater was picking up. I held the alcove curtain open for the duke as he stepped out onto the balcony with me and settled into one of the velvet chairs. There were four in all, and I imagined they more often entertained fancy couples who appreciated operas and ballets—and not fanged snobs who enjoyed a good witch hunt.

"Sit," Dante said, patting the seat beside him. "Let us pretend that you are my scion. Allow me to offer a rudimentary lesson that will impress your pending sire."

The baited suggestion irked me, but I remembered his warning about public acts of disrespect and sat down. I could still see most of the gallery below where guests were arriving and finding their seats, and several decorated vampires soon dotted the balconies across the way from us.

A tall woman with bronze skin and ice-blond hair entered stage left, passing the paneled booth and time-out chair, her red high heels clicking with purpose. The plunging neckline of her blazer exposed far more cleavage than seemed appropriate for a courtroom, and her matching black pencil skirt was tight enough that even the women in the room couldn't help but gawk. She claimed the front center chair of the section I assumed was reserved for the council judges.

Dante angled his head over my shoulder. "That is Lady Regina Beauclair of the Beauclair Corporation. Her house owns a few hundred hotels and resorts all over the world. Their customer base is mostly human, but not exclusively. They have two hotels in St. Louis, though using either for the trial would have been a conflict of interest. It appears she will be leading the hearing."

I dipped my chin in an appreciative nod as the theater filled with more faces I didn't recognize. My attention snagged on a man with a sweep of auburn hair next as he made his way to the stage. His attire was less startling but still pristine and stylish. He unbuttoned his jacket as he took a seat in the armchair to the right of the tartlet in charge.

"Lord Everett Carter. He oversees the vampiric banking systems," Dante said. "And that one is Lady Louise Peyroux." He pointed out an ebony-skinned woman with short, tight curls in a lace blouse and wide-legged dress pants. "She travelled here from Oregon, where her house operates a botanical garden and a large wolfsbane farm."

I recognized the white kung fu jacket of the next vampire to make his way to the dais. We'd met once before.

"Lord Bo Starling," Dante whispered.

"Medical industry and health labs," I injected.

"You know Lord Starling?" His startled surprise made me blush.

"Only *of* him. Through Sonja. We trained together for three months. And Lord Starling was at the All Hallows' Eve ball. I offered him my condolences."

"Is that…the only time your paths crossed?"

"Yes, of course. How else would I know him?"

Dante exhaled slowly. "You are full of surprises, and I have come to dread discovering them."

Well, that wasn't a very nice thing to say.

"They haven't all been bad surprises, have they? I *did* save the queen. And aren't you *glad* to know who your true enemy is now?" I asked.

"If only it was just the one," Dante muttered under his breath. I could tell he struggled to keep a neutral expression, but the wrinkle forming between his eyebrows gave him away as he glanced over the room. "I meant no offense, my dear. I appreciate your insights and gifts. I only wish that my discovery of them did not always coincide with catastrophe."

Okay. That was a fair point.

"What about Rico Suave there?" I asked, hooking my chin at a tall man with long, dark hair and a short beard. He paused to greet the red-heeled vixen and dropped a kiss on her knuckles before taking the seat angled behind her and Lady Peyroux.

"Lord Nicoli DeAngelo." Dante's voice flattened. "Italian architect. His house does a lot of projects for the Beauclair Corporation."

"Is that not a conflict of interest?" I asked.

"Not conflicting enough." Dante sighed. "Many of the elite houses have working relationships. Peyroux supplies Sorano with wolfsbane for their ammunition, and nearly a third of vampire society banks with Carter."

"Is my account with him?" I asked.

"Yes, of course." He cracked a small smile as another vampire claimed the chair between Lord Starling and Lord DeAngelo. "And I would wager everyone here owns at least one armored vehicle manufactured by Lord Owen McCoy's house. The royal family owns dozens of them, and I commissioned him to design the most recent fleet for Blood Vice."

"What's with the red cloaks?" I asked, noting how everyone in the audience wore them, too.

"They represent solidarity and acceptance of the council's decision," Dante said. "The white cloaks represent those sworn to carry out that decision."

One seat in the jury corner remained. As the final councilor took the stage, the duke sucked in a tight breath.

The waifish woman wore a navy jumpsuit and matching stilettos that looked straight off a runway. A shock of lavender hair grazed her white fur vest, and she sported matching lipstick and fingernail polish. She shot Lord Starling a wary glance before taking her place at the opposite end of the back row.

"And she would be?" I whispered.

"Lady Wilhelmina Novak." Dante rubbed a hand over his jaw and sighed. "I somehow doubt she has forgotten House

Lilith's false imprisonment of her house's fledgling scion."

The audience grew louder, and then their voices cut off abruptly as the queen appeared in a balcony off the opposite wall from us. Dante stood, and I followed his lead without having to be told. He waited for Lili's gaze to pause on him, and then we both bowed to her. The guests below us did the same.

After the elaborate All Hallows' Eve ball, the one and only time I'd met the queen, I mistakenly assumed that she always dressed as if she'd just stepped out of the middle ages. But tonight she wore a modern, black ball gown beneath a red cloak that looked no different than anyone else's. She'd even left her crown at home, though her dark hair had been woven into braids that paid tribute to her regality.

Two guards stood on the balcony with the queen, and as the curtains closed behind her, I noticed at least four more blocking off the alcove in the corridor beyond. Though she looked well, I could imagine her people were on high alert after the attack last fall.

A moment later, in a balcony not far from the queen's, Alexander and Kassandra arrived, the most fashionably late of all. The young duchess scanned the crowd, and then her eyes roamed upward until they found Dante and me. I felt the urge to pull up the hood of my cloak and hide from her view.

"If you cannot manage a smile, then at least don't make

eye contact," Dante said through clenched teeth. "We must exercise caution."

I dropped my gaze back to the council judges as they all stood, thankful for the diversion. Ursula was led out and to the chair in the center of the stage. The duchess sat down, but she held her chin high, refusing to crumble under the audience's judging stare. Arrogance didn't seem like a smart choice, but then again, shame and guilt wouldn't have been much better. She was screwed either way.

Lady Beauclair clapped her hands together and offered the room a wide, vicious smile.

"Shall we begin?"

Chapter Ten

"Ursula, Duchess of House Lilith, stands accused of murdering her sire, Morgan, Princess of House Lilith," Lady Beauclair announced. "She also stands accused of unleashing two corrupt, vampling scions on the world. The Vampiric High Council is called here tonight to determine her guilt or innocence, and to exact appropriate punishment for her crimes."

"By the blood!" the crowd cheered, a communal granting of permission to get things started.

It sounded more like something to be yelled at a gladiator match where opponents fought to the death, and it seemed to energize Lady Beauclair. She paced the stage in her clicky red heels and stopped a few feet away from where Ursula sat in the chair of guilt and disgrace. The four white cloaks who had delivered the duchess stood in a line against the backdrop curtains, and more formed a barrier before the front row of the audience. In the shadows at the edge of the stage, I spotted Murphy and Donnie, keeping watch over the duchess as the duke had instructed.

"How do you plead?" Lady Beauclair asked Ursula.

"I'm of House Lilith. I do not plead," she said, hiking her chin farther into the air. "But I will tell you that I am not responsible for the princess's death. I loved Morgan, and I would not have harmed her for anything in the world."

"Do you deny that you were jealous of her potential scion?"

"Of course I was," Ursula snapped. "Every firstborn worries they will be replaced by their sire's newest child."

Dante tensed beside me, and my eyes involuntarily darted across the theater to where Kassandra sat beside the prince. I wondered if he'd felt that way about her when she came along fifty years after him. Was he jealous of his sire's affection for his sibling scion?

"Did you murder your sire's second chosen heir?" Beauclair asked.

"No, I did not." Ursula swallowed and focused her gaze on the councilors. "I was jealous, but I would not harm someone Morgan cared for. I could never cause her such pain."

"If you are not guilty, then why did you flee Morgan's estate in California?" Beauclair demanded.

Ursula readjusted herself on the chair and crossed her legs. The act was meant to project confidence, but the glassy sheen of her eyes broke the illusion. "My sire had just been murdered, our entire harem slaughtered. I was afraid for my life and didn't know whom I could trust. My scions had already defected, but I was in no condition to nurture them back into the fold. So I took the required time to grieve, and then I began my search for them. Unfortunately, Blood Vice was always one step ahead, and I never did catch up with my children."

Beauclair nodded in mock sympathy. "And where is the princess's almost-scion now? Her body was not found among the carnage you left behind."

"She escaped with me," Ursula confessed. "Obviously, she feared for her life, too. We helped each other through the worst of our grief, and then parted ways."

"How convenient." Beauclair smirked. "If only she were here to confirm your fairy tale."

"I am."

The crowd buzzed with whispers and gasps as someone in the back of the theater stood. She walked down the center aisle, pausing just shy of the wall of white cloaks, and pushed back the hood of her robe.

I hardly recognized Annie Miller. She looked nothing like she had a week and a half ago when Mandy and I tricked her into leading us to Ursula's safehouse. Her brunette waves were streaked with gray, and fine lines tightened the planes of her face.

"Let her pass," Beauclair ordered.

Two of the council wardens turned sideways, opening a narrow path so she could reach the stage stairs. Beauclair directed Annie to the paneled booth to the left of the stage, and I surmised that was the designated spot for witness testimonies.

Ursula did not look thrilled to see her former accomplice. I couldn't decide if she was worried about the woman's safety or if the duchess feared she might offer the council some damning detail about their history. Beauclair didn't seem happy she was there either, though I imagined her disdain had more to do with not being able to pin that death on Ursula, too.

"State your name and title for the council," she ordered Annie.

"Heather Anne Miller, former potential scion to Morgan, Princess of House Lilith," Annie said.

"You are aware of the price to have your mortal voice received by the council?"

"I am."

"Annie, no!" Ursula tried to stand, but two of the white cloaks pushed her back down on her chair. "You don't have to do this."

Annie gave her a sad smile. "It's the only thing left for me to do."

A tender, heartbreaking look passed between the women. I'd seen a similar exchange the night Ursula was captured, the way she'd let Annie go as if it were for her own good. Later, at the duke's manor, her hostility toward Annie had been an act to set her free before anyone realized who she was. There was none of that pretense tonight. It was too late for it now.

Beauclair cleared her throat and tapped one of her red heels on the stage floor. This trial was no longer headed toward the gruesome end I could tell she'd been pining after. Her eager plans were about to be demolished, and everyone could tell. Still, Ursula's resistance confused me.

"Do you confirm that the duchess is not responsible for the princess's death?" Beauclair asked.

"I do," Annie said. "She was with me on the beach. Morgan had sent us there together, hoping we might bond before the ceremony. When we returned home…we found our world in ruin."

"Do you have anything else to contribute before your words are sealed in blood?"

I was about to turn to Dante to ask what that entailed when his hand closed over mine.

"It is not right, but it is the way things are done," he said. "Whatever your feelings are on the matter, here and now is not the time to express them."

My eyes went back to the stage in time to watch as one of the council wardens approached Annie. He unsheathed a dagger at his hip, and my heart leapt as I fought not to scream out a warning. When he offered her the handle of the blade, a small sigh of relief slipped from my lips.

Annie offered Ursula one last smile as she took the dagger. Then she angled the tip of it over her chest and used her opposite fist to drive it home into her heart.

Dante's hold on my hand tightened until I remembered to breathe again.

"Her word is now sealed in blood," he whispered in my ear. "Ursula is safe from the charge of Morgan's death."

I couldn't find my voice yet, but I managed to dip my chin in a stiff nod.

Annie had known what she was doing, but it didn't make it any less horrifying. I had to think that Morgan would have been proud of her—and of Ursula—for how much they'd come to care for one another. It seemed such a waste for that bond to end in such a way.

The duchess trembled as she watched a council warden carry Annie's body from the stage. The vampire cradled her in his arms, and a thin trail of blood trickled down the front of his white cloak, spilling from the fatal wound in Annie's chest. The dagger had not been removed yet, its ornate hilt pointing up at the ceiling.

Beauclair turned back to the audience and flipped her icy locks over her shoulder. "On to the second charge, and the most concerning in my humble opinion," she said. "Are you aware of your scions' many, *many* crimes since your…leave of absence?"

Ursula scoffed, but it sounded close to a sob. She'd just witnessed the only friend she'd had for the past twenty years offer up her life to save Ursula from whatever pain and suffering the council hoped to inflict.

"They do not commit their crimes at my behest," she said. "I've not had contact with them since Morgan's death."

"The Vampiric High Council will consider your claim, but only if you produce your scions to receive judgment at this time."

Ursula rolled her eyes up to meet Beauclair's vindictive stare. "I told you that I searched for my scions, but I did not find them."

"You possess the Eye of Blood, do you not?"

The duchess inhaled sharply. "You cannot mean for me to use my sire's death blessing to betray my heirs."

"But I do," Beauclair said. "Unless you are willing to accept the consequences of their crimes in their stead?"

Ursula's breath labored furiously, but she did not have a reply. Her shoulders sagged, and desperation sharpened her features. I'd used the Eye of Blood as freely as a parlor trick to soothe my boredom, and here she was, refraining from using it at all, as if it were a finite talent meant only to honor her late sire.

"The council will recess until tomorrow evening," Beauclair announced to the audience. "This will give the accused the required time to blood call her scions for judgment."

"By the blood!" the crowd cried out, officially ending the session.

Dante remained seated, his broody brow casting a shadow over his eyes as Ursula was led off stage, and the audience began to disperse. I guessed that they were either locals or had made arrangements to stay in one of House Beauclair's hotels for the duration of the trial.

"What's a blood call?" I asked Dante, leaning closer so he could hear me over the din of bloodthirsty spectators. He regarded me with surprise as if he'd forgotten he wasn't alone on the balcony.

"It is a ritual that allows a vampire who possesses the Eye of Blood to compel their scion or scions to come to them," he said.

And just like that, the situation went from bad to worse. I considered biting my tongue, but I *had* promised to help him protect the duchess, and I intended to earn his royal favors fair and square.

"Then I suppose this is a bad time to tell you that Ursula *might* not be Scarlett's sire."

"Hell have mercy." He turned in his seat and covered his face with one hand. "Did Ms. Starling happen to tell you whether or not it is possible for a vampire to die from heart failure?"

Chapter Eleven

Dante waited to resume our conversation until after we'd left the theater hall and had been ushered by a pair of white cloaks to the floor reserved for the royal family. The suites for the duke and duchess were located on one side of the hallway, with those prepared for the queen, prince, and Kassandra at the opposite end. The harem donors were given the rooms closest to the elevators and ice machines in the middle.

We arrived before everyone else, and to Lane's disappointment, the duke stationed him out in the hallway with orders to knock as soon the duchess was delivered to her room. I wasn't looking forward to the awkward explanation I could tell Dante was eager to drag out of me.

"Whatever would give you such a blasphemous idea?" he hissed as we retreated farther inside the suite and hopefully away from any keen ears.

"Scarlett bit me during the raid at the farmhouse last summer," I said. "Wasn't it in the report? I was sure I was questioned by—um—about it."

"By Agent Knight, I presume?" He heaved an annoyed sigh. "I have reviewed his case files as far back as March of last year, and they are rather lacking in detail where you are concerned. It is as if he intentionally left out pertinent information or altered it to downplay your involvement. Why would he do such a thing for a vampling he hardly knew?"

I didn't want to talk about Roman, and certainly not with the asshat who had snapped his neck right in front of me. This was not a conversation I would ever be ready for. It felt as if all my secrets were falling around me as quickly as a house of cards in an earthquake.

"After Scarlett bit me,"—I said, skipping backward over Dante's rude detour—"she just *knew* that Raphael was my sire. She obviously has the Eye of Blood. Which must mean that someone other than Ursula sired her, right? Some other heir of House Lilith who happens to be dead?"

"This is not good." He raked a hand through his hair, and his voice dropped to a hoarse whisper. "The duchess was not ready for a scion, let alone two."

"I don't think that's much of a secret."

"But to be fair," he said, pausing to give me a reprimanding scowl. "It was not something she asked for. She would have been content to live out her days scion-free as long as she had Morgan."

"Seriously. Not a secret." I stared back at him. "I know she was ordered to create a scion. I *did* have a case file on her, remember?"

The uber vampling treatment was beginning to annoy me. I hadn't risen yesterday.

"Scarlett and Raphael were brother and sister as humans,"

Dante said. A haughty grin lit his face when he realized he'd finally gotten me. "You do not know everything. How about this? Ursula sired Raphael first, and his sister a short time later. The queen gave her blessing, though it was an odd request, considering Ursula's initial resistance. At the time, Ursula told me that Raphael had begged, and she took pity on him. Though perhaps she simply did not wish to admit how depraved her new vamplings were."

"You don't think that…" My skin crawled at the thought of Raphael and Scarlett sharing blood. It just seemed…wrong. "Ew."

"I think Ursula suspects." Dante sighed and shook his head.

"You think? She looked ready to piss herself when Lady Butt Hair ordered her to blood call them."

Dante covered his mouth, but the corners of his eyes crinkled with amusement. "I should warn you, if you ever say that to her face, she would be within her rights to challenge you to a blood duel."

"I know, I know," I said, waving him off. "Vampires don't piss or engage in any other *shameful* human activities."

"I meant your pet name for Beauclair."

"If I ever come face-to-face with that woman, *I'll* be the one pissing myself."

He nodded. "She chills my blood, as well."

"So. What's going to happen to Ursula when she does this blood call thing, and no one shows up?"

"That is the question." Dante peeled off his cloak and tossed it over a chair angled in front of a desk in the corner. Then he touched a finger to his chin and squinted at me. "Perhaps being Scarlett's grandsire will be enough. We shall see."

"We shall, shall we?" I folded my arms and cocked a brow at him. "You don't think Scarlett showing up and bumping into *me* will be…problematic?"

I could just see it now. The little twat's eyes would well with tears as she pointed an accusing finger, dubbing me Raphael's murderer and scion in one. Then, the council would have a third victim to crucify—a third victim from House Lilith, no less.

"Pull up the hood of your cloak," Dante said. I bristled at his commanding tone but did as he instructed, pushing my braid behind my shoulders. "In the dim light of the theater, that should suffice."

He couldn't be serious. All Scarlett would have to do is fire up her blood vision, and then the world would be her brightly lit, bloody oyster. A strange realization hit me.

"You don't have the Eye of Blood. You don't really know what all it entails, do you?"

"I am most certainly aware of what gifts the eye bestows,

Ms. Skye." Dante's shoulders squared as if he were offended by the very idea that I might have some advantage over him—an advantage that was far more his birthright than mine. "If you think the hood is not enough, you are welcome to trade places with Lane and cower behind the balcony curtains."

"Wonderful," I shot back at him. "Then *he* can hold your hand the next time a witness commits harikari."

Dante's lips parted, and I saw the tips of his fangs drop a fraction lower than the rest of his pearly whites. We were both on edge and running out of solutions to a seemingly never-ending problem. Before he could bite back at me, Lane knocked on the door.

"The duchess has been delivered to her quarters, Your Grace," his muffled voice called out. "The queen and prince, as well."

"Good. Thank you," Dante replied, eyes still fixed on me. His fangs retracted, and the scowl creasing his face softened until he'd regained the air of effortless authority I was more accustomed to.

It was becoming easier to get under his skin, and though it did me no favors, I reveled in the achievement. I would have enjoyed it even more if my life weren't hanging so precariously in the balance.

"I must properly greet my sire. You will be staying in Ursula's suite," Dante said with equal relief and concern. "Try not to goad her into slaughtering you. Her night has been troublesome enough."

"Yes, Your Grace." I pinched the folds of my cloak and held it out to either side as I paid him a mocking curtsey.

"And have some blood soon," he added. "You are more tolerable when you're well fed."

He stalked from the room before I could think of a witty retort. As I stepped out into the hallway, Lane and I both turned to watch the duke storm off toward the prince's suite.

"Murph says you're the one who finally found the duchess," Lane said under his breath. "That true?"

"I had help." Considering all the hell that had followed, I didn't feel the need to take full credit for the feat.

"Well, I don't blame you for not wanting to testify—if that's what the boss is trying to get you to do." He gave me a sympathetic frown. "The day I seal my word in blood will be the day the council seals my ass with a kiss."

"The duke hasn't asked me to testify. Yet." I wondered if it would come to that and how he'd take it when I responded the same way Lane just had. I could count the people I'd lay down my life for on one hand, and Ursula was not among them.

As if she'd read my mind, a muffled shriek of outrage and the sound of something shattering against a wall came from her suite. Then, Murphy and Donnie were suddenly in the hallway with us.

"She's all yours," Murphy said, holding the door wide open. "I'll go tell your wolf to get a blood pot together and head this way. Keep an eye out till then—she's been working on her curveball."

"Super." I sighed and entered the domain of Ursula's temper tantrum. Murphy closed the door behind me, barricading the cyclone of her wrath.

Inside the suite, the duchess paced before the window. Her lace dress and red curls reflected in a blur across the glass, breaking up the St. Louis skyline in the distance. The industrial light created an imposter dawn that backlit the clouds. Sunrise was at least six hours off. I loathed the idea of spending that much time trapped in a room with Ursula.

"I don't care what arrangements Dante has made," she hissed. "You will not be staying in this room with me. It is *your* fault I'm here in the first place."

"I was following the duke's orders, the same as I am now." I folded my arms and leaned against the doorframe. With the busted glass on the floor and the warpath she was treading between the beds and the window, it seemed the safest place to camp out.

"Did you enjoy watching Annie die, vampling?"

"I liked Annie," I admitted. I hadn't cared for the way she manhandled Mandy at the duchess's safehouse, but she had also hoodwinked Arnie Moreau and roughed up one of his goons in her quest to find Scarlett and Raphael. She was tough and loyal, and she'd given her life for someone she loved—even if that someone was a hateful old bat.

"Liar!" Ursula picked up a ceramic bauble from the bedside table and heaved it across the room. It narrowly missed my head and smashed against the wall to the left of the door. Despite my effort to put on a brave face, I flinched as a shard scraped my cheek.

"I liked her a hell of a lot more than I like you right now," I said, glowering at the duchess.

She reached for another knickknack, but there were none left. From the remains on the floor, I could see that she'd already taken care of a music box, a vase of white roses, and the unfortunate figurine she'd aimed at me—a fairy or butterfly, I guessed from a colorful bit of ceramic shaped like a monarch's forewing.

"Look what you've made me do?" Ursula spat.

"My deepest apologies, Your Grace." I hiked a thumb over my shoulder. "Would you like me to go fetch the trinkets from the duke's room so you can have a go with those, too?"

"I will rip out your insolent throat!" She stalked across the room, arms outstretched and fingers curling.

The door swung open behind me, and I jerked around, unprepared to find the queen standing there. Ursula's surprise trumped my own. She gasped and retreated a step, clenching her fists to her chest while I backed into the corner between the desk and door and pretended I was invisible.

Lili had removed the red cloak, revealing lace—see-through sleeves that drew a gothic pattern down her arms. The bodice cut a flat line across her breastbone, and above the material throbbed a blue vein that disappeared up the column of her neck. In one hand she held a sheathed dagger, and I had a moment of panic, wondering if she intended for one of us to make use of it the way Annie had.

Two of the queen's guards lingered in the hall, but they did not follow as she entered the room and closed the door behind her. She paid no attention to me as she approached the duchess. I was nothing more than a royal guard tonight. Saving her life—the life of anyone in House Lilith—was no longer a noble gesture worthy of praise, but part of my job description.

"Your Majesty." Ursula dropped to her knees. "I beg you, spare my errant children—"

"Rise," the queen snapped. Ursula obeyed, standing instantly. "You could have come to me twenty years ago before the council demanded such involvement, and I would have gladly aided you."

"I couldn't—" Ursula closed her eyes and choked back a sob. "Not after…"

"Morgan was my first scion," the queen said. "I grieved for her, too, but I did not abandon my family. Now, your children have been sullied by the world. They are untamed and out of control. Ridiculed, reviled, and no longer fit to rule. You will call them to you, and you will accept whatever judgment the council passes on them without resistance. Do you understand, Ursula?"

"Yes, Your Majesty," she whispered.

The queen took Ursula's hand and pressed the dagger into it. "Do this for me, for our family, and I will keep you from harm. Fail, and *I* will accept the council's judgment on *you.*"

The queen's eyes migrated across the room toward me, and I made a point to lower my gaze and bow my head. I heard the door open and close, and when I looked up, I was alone in the room with Ursula.

The duchess held the sheathed dagger in both hands, regarding it with a pinched brow. Her eyes brimmed with tears, and then, as if remembering that I was there, she tossed the blade onto one of the beds and stalked back toward the window.

"Can't you do…whatever it is you're doing just as well from the hallway?"

"I'd love to." I turned and headed for the exit. "Surely one of the other guards is just *dying* to bear witness to your vampy telepathic ritual and then seal it in blood for the council."

Before I reached the door, Ursula was on my back, ripping me farther inside the room. Her hand slapped over my mouth, her thumb and forefinger pinching around my nose as I thrashed against her. The Eye of Blood painted the room red with my panic.

"On second thought, vampling, why don't you stick around?" she said, her breath rushing out in a desperate pant. "I'd much rather christen the eye on your secrets than my scions' ruin."

My fingernails scratched and clawed at my face as I tried to pry her off, and my muffled screams went unheard. This was not happening. This *couldn't* be happening.

Ursula's free hand clasped my shoulder, and she spun me around, pushing my back against the wall. Reason had abandoned her, and a wild arrogance filled her gaze. I recognized the look—I'd seen it before in the eyes of her scions.

With one hand still smothering my face, she wrenched my arm up and sank her fangs into the pit of my wrist, scraping bones and nerve endings. There was nothing gentle about her bite. I'd been attacked by dogs with more decorum.

My blood flowed freely, and with it, an ugly truth that could destroy us both.

Chapter Twelve

"Raphael," Ursula gasped, caught in a memory that wasn't hers. "No. *Don't*."

My blood dripped from her fangs and bottom lip, spilling onto the pale lace of her dress. I couldn't see how much was revealed to her, but I could guess.

My death had been messy. Remembering it roused phantom pains in the bend of my neck—agony I knew Ursula now felt, thanks to the Eye of Blood and the way it bequeathed the memory of a mortal passing in its entirety.

The duchess's shoulders trembled, and her face twisted with agony as she wilted to the floor. She leaned over her bent knees and sobbed. The sound was an echo of the noise I'd made in the warehouse basement as I took my final breaths. It made me feel vulnerable and pathetic all over again.

I gripped my wrist where Ursula had bitten me and slid my back along the wall, using it for support as I tried to put some distance between us. I didn't want to be within easy reach once the vision released her. I didn't want to be in the same *country*.

In the short time I'd known her, the duchess had proven to be unhinged and unpredictable. There was no telling how she'd take the news of Raphael being my sire. I somehow doubted a tender family reunion was in the cards.

"Then it's true." Her eyes refocused and snapped to me, freezing my progress toward the door. "But it was clearly an accident. Your existence is purely accidental. Dumb luck." She let out a dry laugh. "I suppose that sums you up, doesn't it?"

"I'll take dumb luck over willful ignorance any day," I said, cradling my wrist to my chest. Blood smeared across the slick material of my catsuit as I balled up the hem of my cloak and attempted to staunch the flow. If I survived the night, I would have to find out if the theater had a laundering service.

A knock sounded at the door, but before I could call out a warning, it opened. Dante took in the scene with wide eyes, and then his head jerked to the side, and he threw out his hand.

"You will have to come back later," he said.

"I was told to come now." I heard Mandy huff. "What am I supposed to do with this blood?"

"Put it on a hot plate," Dante snapped. Then he slipped into the room and slammed the door behind him, flipping the deadbolt so that no one with a key card could barge in unannounced.

The smashed baubles on the floor and the blood smeared across Ursula's face seemed to confuse him. It made me wonder if he were trying to decide how the two were related, but then he did a double-take at the wad of cloak coiled around my wrist, and understanding lit his eyes with horror.

"What have you done?" he hissed at me.

"Me?" I glared at him and lifted my injured wrist. "What have *I* done?"

"She is too fragile right now," Dante said as if I'd somehow forced Ursula to bite me.

"You knew." Ursula's attention shifted from me to the duke, and her eyes filled with black like a mushroom cloud engulfing the sky after an atomic bomb. "How could you keep such a thing from me?"

Dante held up his hands as she rose. "It is complicated, cousin—"

"Don't you *cousin* me," she snarled. "Does the queen know—no. Of course she doesn't. The little fiend is still alive, so how could she?"

"Ursula," Dante pleaded, edging away as she advanced on him. "If you'd just let me explain—"

"Explain what?" She laughed maniacally. "How you managed to find me but not Morgan's murderer? Or how you employed my own grandscion to hunt me down like an animal?"

Dante's back hit the wall, and he finally broke free of the recoiling dance he'd been pacifying the duchess with. He took her by the shoulders and matched her venomous glare with one of his own.

"I did not know whom she belonged to at the time," he said, clenching his teeth. "She was a vampling and a new hire. Do you really think I expected her to find you?"

I huffed out an offended noise before I could contain my resentment. It hadn't occurred to me that the duke had been so sure I'd fail to solve my first case. That he'd actually set me up to do so. I would have been proud if I weren't so insulted.

"You know who she is now." Ursula gave him an accusing glare. "So why is she still here? Why haven't you told the queen?"

"Oh, cousin…" Dante blew out an angry sigh and gave her shoulders a gentle shake. "The council wants to punish you on the grounds of being a neglectful sire. Do you suppose unleashing the knowledge that your scion produced an illegitimate vampling will help your cause?"

"Slitting her throat should help with that, no?" Ursula countered, shooting me a vicious look that sent a tremor up my spine.

"Is that what you really want?" he asked. "To see your grandscion—your only blood descendant of any reputable worth—perish?"

The duchess considered his words, conflicting emotions playing out across her delicate face. "If I had more time, I could save Raphael. He could be well again."

"Raphael is dead," Dante confessed. "And I'm well aware

that Scarlett was his."

Ursula's mouth dropped open. Her fangs descended in a panicked hiss as she broke free of his hold and retreated to the window.

She hadn't known. As much as I despised the duchess, my heart bled at her mourning. She cupped her hands over her mouth to stifle her sobs, and her curls trembled against the lace back of her dress.

"You should be glad that your grandscion is here." Dante crept up behind her, slowly resting his hands on her shoulders again. It was a comforting touch this time that he delivered with a soothing voice. "She possesses the eye, as well. Together, you should be able to blood call Scarlett. It is your only hope of leaving here of your own free will, cousin."

"The council will not be satisfied until I'm locked in a coffin." Ursula's voice seeped resigned melancholy.

"Call Scarlett," Dante said, rubbing slow circles on her back and shoulders. His tired eyes sought me out across the room. "And have faith. Your grandscion is quite the lucky charm."

It was all I could do to keep from begging the duke to take me with him when he left. Though the worst of Ursula's mood seemed to have passed, she was no picnic to be around, and I had no idea how this blood call was supposed to work or what would be expected of me.

Ursula sat down on the bed she'd left the queen's dagger on and picked it up. Then she motioned for me to hand her my cloak.

"Yours is already mucked up," she said. "No sense in bloodying mine, as well."

I stripped out of the robe and tossed it across the room, earning an annoyed grunt when it nearly hit her in the face. The ragged holes in my wrist were raw, but they'd begun to crust over. I was sure my morning blood intake would heal the worst of the damage, but I still regarded the duchess with cautious skepticism as I joined her on the bed, leaving plenty of space between us.

"So, what's the blade for?" I asked. "Do you rub it like a lamp? Spit on it for good luck?"

"This is Lilith's ceremonial blade." Ursula gaped at me in horror. "It's been used in the creation of every scion of House Lilith since the beginning of time—well, except for *you*."

"And any other grandbastards you might have out there stalking the night."

She harrumphed and unsheathed the dagger. "It's a *blood* call. What do you think we're going to do with it?"

"Use the tip to punch in Scarlett's phone number?" It was

unlikely, but I wasn't ready to cave just yet. I greened at the idea of letting her anywhere near me with yet another sharp, pointy object.

"Don't be such a baby fangs." She huffed and snatched my hand, dragging the blade across my palm without warning. I winced as my skin opened, but before I could examine the new wound, Ursula slashed her own palm and pressed it to mine, clasping our hands together. I made a gagging face, and she loosed another exasperated sigh.

"We should have at least *tried* rubbing it first, don't you think?"

"Pay attention," she snapped. "We don't have all night, vampling."

"Really? That's a relief." Playing bloody pat-a-cake with Granny Long Fangs was not what I'd had in mind for my evening agenda.

"It's easy." She dialed down her patronizing tone so I'd hear *what* she said and not just *how* she said it. "Repeat after me, only replace the 'child of my child' bit with 'child of my sire.' Make sense? Can you do that?"

"We'll see," I said, hoping like hell I didn't botch the ritual. I really didn't want *both* hands getting sliced and diced if we had to do a second take.

"Child of Lilith, child of my child, heed my call in your blood this night," Ursula chanted. I waited for her to say something more, but when she only stared intently at me, I realized it was my turn.

"Oh! Child of Lilith…child of my *sire*…heed my call in your blood this night?" I echoed.

Ursula's hand tightened around mine, and our thickening blood tickled my palm as it worked its way down to my ravaged wrist and dripped onto my outstretched cloak.

I kept waiting for some sparkling, firework effect. Some sizzle or zap to shoot through my veins and let me know our mojo was working. But nothing happened.

"How long do we have to hold hands like this?" I whispered.

"Shhh." Ursula gave me a sharp look and then closed her eyes as if concentrating. I tried to do the same, picturing Scarlett's hateful face. Maybe that would help. The exercise was grating, and I soon grew bored.

"What if Raphael sired more than just Scarlett and me?" I asked. "What if a whole army of vampires shows up when attendance is called tonight?"

"*Shhh.*" Ursula reprimanded me. "If you never speak again, it will be too soon."

I waited another few moments before I couldn't take it anymore.

"You said we didn't have all night, and I'm hungry and bleeding." I hated how whiny I sounded, but either the blood call would work, or it wouldn't. One way or the other, I needed blood, and at least ten more feet of personal space. Stat.

Ursula squeezed my hand tighter until I yelped, and then she released me. "Call for our morning *tea* and clean yourself up. You reek of stale blood."

"And whose fault is that?" I snapped as I yanked my cloak off the bed and clenched it in my palm to stop the bleeding.

Ursula ignored me. She placed her own hand in her lap and studied the gash in her palm as if reading her future. *Extra-long lifeline. Broken heart line. Blood line straight from hell.*

"Heed my call in your blood this night." She whispered the words in a despairing prayer, over and over until guilt sucker punched me.

I slumped to the bed and timidly slipped my hand back into hers. Ursula's eyes met mine, but whatever hope she had was quickly fading. She didn't even rebuke me as I altered the wording of her plea.

"Heed *our* call in your blood this night," we chanted. The droning harmony of our voices increased with each pass. It was almost…soothing. I felt myself drift into a trance.

Scarlett was out there somewhere. Ursula didn't seem as attached to her as she was to Raphael, but it made sense. She wasn't Scarlett's true sire, and the girl was pure, psychotic evil. As much as the thought of seeing her again terrified me, I did hope she *heeded* our call.

And I hoped it was the last call she ever answered.

Chapter Thirteen

The long-distance blood call to Scarlett took longer than I would have preferred, but it didn't last all night. Thank goodness. Ursula was a tough one to pity for long, considering her winning personality. After we'd finally called it quits, she slunk off to the bathroom to shower while I buzzed the harem room Mandy was in and asked her to come back with our blood—and my overnight bag. I was ready to get out of the catsuit and into pajamas.

As I waited, I picked up the broken bits of ceramic and glass from the floor and deposited them in the tiny trash bin under the desk. No one needed to find any of that in the bottom of their foot. Then I snapped the stems of the white roses down to size and placed them in a paper cup I found near a coffeemaker. The room was put back to rights by the time Mandy arrived, though she didn't rely on her eyes alone to sense trouble.

"Why do I smell *your* blood?" she asked as I greeted her.

"The duchess was ordered to perform a ritual—" I gave her a tight-lipped smile as my eyes darted to the closed bathroom door. "Let's just say that Scarlett may or may not be dropping in for night two of the trial."

"What?" Mandy shoved my duffel bag at me and hurried inside the room, closing the door behind her. She set the tray with the blood pot and the hotel coffee cups down on the night table and put her hands on her hips. "Come again?"

"It's a little hard to explain right now," I whispered as the sound of the showerhead cut off. "But you'll be safe and sound in the harem suite, so chill."

Mandy's chest rose and fell rapidly as if she were on the verge of hyperventilating. "Chill?" she scoffed, then her eyes dropped to my hand pressed against my stomach, the damaged side hidden from view. "I'll bite her face clean off—"

"It was voluntary." I snatched her arm as she turned for the bathroom and gave her a pleading look, hoping she refrained from asking more questions. "I'll fill you in once this is all over and we're back at the manor. Cross my heart. Just…keep it on the DL for now, okay?"

Mandy huffed and ripped off her cloak. She tossed it down beside the bed and began stripping off her catsuit next.

"What what *what* are you doing?" I dropped the duffel bag and pressed my un-maimed hand to my forehead.

"I'm shifting," she snapped. "You want me to *chill?* You want things on the *DL?* This is the only way I'm keeping my mouth shut around Big Bad Red until sunrise."

"*Uuuugh.* Okay. Fine." I turned around, more to spare my eyes than her modesty. Mandy had none.

The sound of bones and sinew realigning sent up the hairs

on the back of my neck. Shifting was painful. Mandy didn't have to spell that out for me. I didn't even have to see her do it. Being torn apart and put back together in a different order made the kind of noises I expected a body to make if it were being crushed like a soda can.

When I turned around, Mandy was fully changed. Her yellow eyes stared at me through black and brown fur. The lighter color also tipped her tail that sliced through the air behind her as she jumped onto the bed closest to the door— the one I'd be resting in for the day.

Ursula stepped out of the bathroom in a gray silk pajama set. She stopped towel drying her hair to glare at Mandy. "Doesn't this hotel have a no-pet policy?"

Mandy growled in warning, but quickly stopped when I shot her a dirty look. Leaving them alone together was not a great idea, but between the nervous sweating and the crusty blood, I desperately needed a shower. I attempted a smile at Ursula. Sharing a bloody handshake hadn't made us besties by any means, but it had to count for something.

"If someone breaks in here during the day, you'll be glad she's in her strongest form," I said, bending over to fetch my duffel bag. I slung it over my shoulder before taking up the blood pot and filling the pair of coffee cups. Hopefully, that would keep her happy and quiet long enough for me to get cleaned up. And, hopefully, it would heal up my injuries, too.

I cradled a cup in each hand and crossed the room, giving one of them to Ursula before slipping past her and into the bathroom with mine.

"Try not to kill each other while I wash up for bed," I called over my shoulder. "I somehow doubt that will earn any brownie points with the council—and we definitely won't get our deposit back." After Ursula's destructive tantrum, I was betting that we wouldn't get the deposit back regardless, but I'd use any incentive I could to get a few minutes of peace to myself.

With Mandy in the bedroom, and the other two werewolf guards standing watch in the hallway, I wasn't worried about an assassin trying to take out the duchess. I imagined the half-sired agent had taken up a post in the duke's suite, and I was sure there were more guards stationed at the opposite end of the hall for the queen and company. Still, I couldn't relax.

I locked myself in the bathroom and hung the strap of my bag over the hook on the back of the door. The mirror was steamed over from Ursula's lengthy shower. She'd forgotten to turn on the exhaust fan. I considered leaving it off so I could hear if things got out of hand in the bedroom, but then I decided *the hell with it* and flipped the switch.

The noise granted more privacy than the enclosed space, and I finally released a long, aching breath. I cradled the cup of blood in my bum hand and used my other to clear a spot on the mirror, taking in my ashen complexion and frazzled braid. Add in the black catsuit, and I looked like I just escaped a sex dungeon.

I kicked aside a soggy towel Ursula had left on the floor and braced myself against the sink before chugging down the cup of lukewarm blood. A shudder rocked through me, hard enough to make my spine pop, and I set the cup down a little harder than I intended, nearly cracking it on the vanity countertop.

My hand tingled and itched. I turned it over and watched as the skin on my palm and at the bend of my wrist knit itself back together. Red, inflamed marks remained, but a good day's rest would hopefully fix that.

I rinsed the crusted blood off my hands in the sink before peeling out of my catsuit. One of the harem donors would come to collect our laundry after sunrise. I wasn't used to the maid service the royal family took for granted, but at least they paid their help instead of using Jedi mind tricks like the movie vamps.

The hotel shower stall was nice, but I'd expected nothing less from a suite usually reserved for opera divas and ballerinas. Still, I didn't linger. I trusted Mandy more than Ursula to remain civil, but she definitely wouldn't roll over and play dead if things got dicey with the duchess.

When I stepped back into the bedroom in my flannel

pajamas, I was surprised to find Ursula lying on her bed, facing the window. Mandy watched quietly from my bed, her muzzle resting on the tops of her paws, yellow eyes wide and alert. If I'd known they were going to get on this well, I might have lingered longer.

Ursula's back rose and fell heavily—the way a human's might if they'd dozed off. But vampires didn't snooze. They died at dawn and rose at dusk. Any downtime in between was due to critical injury or lack of blood, not a catnap.

"There's another cup of blood in the pot," she said as if she could feel me staring. "You should have it before it gets cold."

"Thanks."

The polite exchange felt awkward, but I wouldn't turn down the extra blood if it were being freely offered. I fetched my cup from the bathroom counter and refilled it at the night table sandwiched between the beds. The drink sent another shudder through me, though not as intensely as the first, even though the blood had lost much of its flavor as it cooled.

Once I'd finished, I climbed onto the bed with Mandy and stretched out. I didn't bother getting under the covers. It wasn't like I'd wake up if I got too cold in the middle of the day. The sun held as much sway over me as the moon held over Mandy.

I spent the remaining moments until sunrise thinking

about the trial and wondering what to expect once it resumed. Lady Beauclair seemed out for blood—in the figurative sense, as well. Something about her persistence and unabashed desire to see Ursula suffer felt…off. Hadn't anyone else noticed? Or was it normal for big-wig vampires to so openly display their bias in a setting that was supposed to be fair?

The other councilors had far better poker faces. I'd committed their names to memory, along with anything else Dante had shared about them. For all I knew, I might find myself adopted into one of their households come summer.

When the sun neared the horizon, my eyelids grew heavy. I reached down to run a hand through Mandy's fur. Just to let her know it was time. She would have to watch over us now. I trusted her with my life—and not just because I had to.

Mandy knew everything there was to know about me, and she was still my friend. The same way I knew everything about her, including some pretty incriminating facts, and yet she hadn't chewed my heart out in my sleep.

We were in this together, and even if the sun didn't force my eyes closed every morning, I knew I wouldn't have had any trouble sleeping with her watching over me. I wondered if Ursula would be winking out with as much confidence, and the thought made me sad for her.

I rolled onto my side and faced her back, noting the way her shoulders cinched up near her ears. She was waiting to die.

Not just for the day, but a true death. Something told me she had been ever since Morgan's murder. That maybe the only thing she was holding on to was the hollow ache of a memory. Or the fading illusion of vengeance.

I'd survived on both not so long ago. Like Morgan's killer, the man who had shot my mother had never been found. Somewhere along the way, I'd found enough purpose to keep going. It didn't look like the duchess had. Not yet anyway.

"Rest well, Your Grace," I said just before my eyes closed and my breath stilled.

"Rest well, vampling," Ursula whispered back, her words floating on the cusp of dawn.

Chapter Fourteen

If someone had told me this time last year that I'd be a royal guard at a vampire trial, I would have called in a 5150 and had the best story to tell over donuts in the morning. As it was, if I told an unenlightened human that I was a royal vampire guard, *I* would be considered the 5150. And, unfortunately, vampires couldn't have donuts.

I was still stewing over that one. I let it roll around in my mind Saturday evening, trying to distract myself from more important concerns as we waited to be summoned back to the theater by the council. There were no reported sightings of Scarlett, and I feared the blood call hadn't worked. Donuts would have certainly made the tension at least a *little* easier to stomach.

Mandy had headed back to the harem to catch up on sleep as soon as the sun set. So it was just Ursula and me, sipping fresh blood and pacing the room in silence. For *hours*.

My catsuit and cloak smelled of lavender detergent. It should have soothed me, but I was wound too tightly. If Scarlett made an appearance, I would do exactly what Dante had snidely suggested and hide behind the balcony curtains. It wasn't purely cowardice. If we were anywhere else, I wouldn't have been able to trust myself not to take the law into my own hands—judge, jury, and executioner style. But surrounded by vampires who could inflict a far worse fate on me, I had to be careful.

A sharp knock made me jump. I set down my empty cup and checked the peephole before opening the door for Dante. He was in another fancy waistcoat tonight. The black-on-black gave it a *Phantom of the Opera* vibe. Murphy, Donnie, and Lane stood behind him, the hoods of their cloaks pulled up over their heads. A shadow shifted across the floor, alerting me that they weren't alone.

I leaned past the threshold and stole a quick glance around the corner. Four white-cloaked guards waited in the hall.

"It is time," Dante said. His jaw flexed as he glanced past me to where Ursula stood in front of the window. "The council has decided that the trial will resume now."

"But it's only midnight," Ursula protested. "My scions could be halfway across the world. They haven't allowed enough time."

"I have told the council as much." Dante sighed. "They are unyielding on the matter. I suggest that you…take all the time you need to answer Lady Beauclair's follow-up questions tonight."

His careful wording was for the council wardens in the hall, I was sure.

Ursula snatched her cloak off the bed and threw it over

her shoulders. She'd chosen a beige dress for night two of the trial. The color was neutral and not half as pretentious as a white dress would have been. The innocent connotation would have been an insult to the council. Ursula had been cleared of Morgan's murder, but there was no denying that she'd been a negligent sire. She wouldn't leave here tonight without paying for that crime.

I followed her from the room, stopping suddenly when Dante held up a hand and nodded for Murphy and Donnie to take over the escort duty. They slipped in on either side of the duchess and followed two of the council wardens. The remaining two filed in behind the entourage.

I fell into step beside Lane, drawing up the hood of my mantle like the other guards. I wondered if Dante had instructed them to do so for my benefit. If it had been an order, I was guessing he hadn't told them why. Lane didn't poke fun at me for being afraid of facing the homicidal brat I'd put out of business, anyway. I nudged his shoulder as we followed the duke back to his reserved balcony.

"Wanna trade places tonight?"

"Nah," he whispered. "I've been to dozens of trials. This is your first. Enjoy it."

Enjoy it? Yeah, right.

My nerves were raw, and my evening blood sat heavily in my stomach. Grim anticipation clouded my mood, but it wasn't my newfound pity for the duchess that filled me with hope that she'd be saved from an extended coffin nap. The duke's promise to keep my sire secret and to help me return to Blood Vice was still at the forefront of my mind.

It seemed a hefty price for what little I'd agreed to do, but simply showing up had negated the more horrifying task of testifying for the council. I'd been dubbed a useless pawn for the defense—even though I'd been the one to track down Ursula. Though it still irked me that the duke hadn't explained the testifying process more thoroughly.

"Did you rest well?" he asked as we settled into the balcony seats. The theater was quickly filling up below, and the murmur of excited voices veiled our conversation.

"I suppose so, especially since I didn't have to seal anything in blood." I gave him a humorless smile, and his eyes widened.

"You thought…" He made to reach for my hand but stopped himself short of touching me as the queen arrived. A second later, the prince and Kassandra entered their balcony across the way from us, too.

The prince nodded to Dante with a subdued but genuine smile. He was a handsome man, if a bit forgettable. I couldn't picture him ever filling the queen's shoes, but maybe there was more to him than met the eye. Kassandra, on the other hand, commanded attention. Her bourbon-colored curls were pinned back away from her face, and deep green eyes lined with kohl drank me in before she offered a small smile of her own to Dante. He returned the look with matched courtesy.

Appearances were important. We couldn't let on that we knew she had tried to assassinate the queen. Which made her suspect *numero uno* in my book for Morgan's death and the attempt on Ursula. But without hard evidence, there wasn't much we could do. Since I was absolutely *not* going to offer myself up to the council on a silver platter.

"Testimony is only sealed in blood if it is offered rather than requested by the council," Dante said, picking up where we'd left off before the rest of the royal family had arrived. "I would never ask that of you."

"That's good to know," I said, adjusting my hood to better hide my flushed cheeks.

The bat cave had covered the most common crimes and punishments, but it had left a lot to be desired when it came to explaining trial proceedings. My ignorance proved more annoying every day. I vowed to spend more time in the library once we returned to the manor.

Showing up for the trial as one of the duke's royal guards had seemingly changed the council's mind to have me testify about Ursula's arrest. It was a smart strategy. I could give Dante that. Though my relief was hinged on doubt.

If the council accused Ursula of defying them and not

performing the ritual, they could very well opt not to call on me to vouch for her. At which point, I had to wonder if Dante would change his tune about me throwing myself on my sword—or some random guard's dagger—to save his beloved cousin.

I'd believe that his intentions were pure just as soon as we were the hell out of here.

The jury councilors began to make their way across the stage to their seats. I paid closer attention to them this time, noting which ones seemed to be friends and which ones might possibly be feuding. It was a tough guessing game, but there were a few tells that I picked up on—and, of course, the previous knowledge of House Starling's and House Novak's sordid history.

Beyond the fancy lords and ladies of high vamp society, in the shadowy recess of the stage, I spotted a coffin lying on a wheeled cart. Two white cloaks stood in front of it, but they did little to hide the terror-inducing prop.

Once Ursula had been delivered to her chair of shame, the theater grew quiet. Beauclair stood and faced the audience, watching as the last few guests settled and the doors in the back were closed. She was dressed a hair more modestly tonight, in a blood-red bolero over a black slip dress. As soon as she had everyone's full attention, she turned to Ursula and folded her hands as if she were about to announce something as cheerfully mundane as bingo numbers.

"I do not see your scions in attendance, Your Ladyship. The council demanded that you call them by blood twenty-four hours ago. Where are they?"

Ursula lifted her chin and glared at the woman. "They could be anywhere in the world. They need more time—"

"We all know they are not *anywhere* in the world," Beauclair scoffed. "Did you even perform the ritual?"

"Of course, I did." Ursula held up her hand to display the pinkish scar dissecting her palm. The same mark that still graced my hand. Lili's blade had been silver, so the wound was taking its sweet time healing.

"In the past twenty years, your scions have committed countless crimes," Beauclair went on, discounting Ursula's claim. "The notorious Scarlett Inn, where they risked exposing not only vampiric society but the werewolf community as well, has stained the reputation of House Lilith. Not to mention the numerous humans who died at their hands, either directly or through drug overdoses and unsavory and illegal transactions with the scum of the shifter underworld. And yet, you did nothing."

"The inn was constantly moving," Ursula snapped. "I *tried*. Annie and I even followed them to Missouri when we heard they'd left Denver."

"Unfortunately, Ms. Miller's blood has already been used

to pardon you for one crime," Beauclair said as if she still suspected that Ursula was guilty of Morgan's murder. A twenty-year-old rumor was hard to shake in one night, I guessed.

The double doors at the back of the theater were suddenly thrown open. They slammed into the walls, and a chorus of surprised hisses echoed throughout the room, making it sound like a snake pit.

A few council members stood, and the audience twisted in their seats to watch two Blood Vice agents I recognized from the St. Louis office haul in a squirming, kicking figure with a canvas sack over her head.

My breath seized in my lungs as they dragged her down the center aisle, and I remained in my seat, too afraid to move for fear of drawing attention. Dante inched forward in his chair and turned more fully toward the stage, offering me his back as cover, and I could suddenly breathe again.

"Thank you," I said over his shoulder. My gratitude was too great for pride right now.

I leaned past Dante just enough to watch as the agents stuffed their bounty inside the witness box where Annie had died the night before. They ripped off the canvas sack, and a collective gasp echoed up from the audience.

It surprised me to see Scarlett in jeans and a hoodie, looking no more dignified than an average, punk teenager caught playing hooky. Of course, it was clever on her part. With Blood Vice hunting her, there was no better disguise than to blend in with the masses. Her cutesy dresses and hair ribbons were a trademark that even a vampling like me was familiar with.

"Did the blood call...work?" I whispered. Dante shrugged and gave me a cocky grin.

"It might have. Though I suppose the bonus I offered to any unit that delivered her to the theater helped speed things along."

"I'd say so."

The agents scanned the room until they found the duke, and they gave him a quick salute, making sure he got a good look at their faces before heading out of the theater the way they'd come in. The white cloaks lined up before the front row traded nervous glances, and then one of them moved to join the guards on stage.

"Did you miss me, Mother?" Scarlett batted her lashes at Ursula. She had to know that Raphael was her true sire—she was perfectly aware of the Eye of Blood she possessed. But I supposed she wouldn't openly admit that to the council. That would make her an unsanctioned scion of the late baron and earn her nothing short of an execution.

Ursula was speechless. Her eyes slid up to where Dante and I sat, but she quickly redirected her gaze. I leaned in closer to the duke, hiding from sight once again.

"Scarlett Lilosa, exiled baroness of House Lilith," Beauclair addressed her. "You are charged with the criminal operations of the Scarlett Inn that risked exposure of our kind and resulted in numerous human and werewolf deaths. How do you plead?"

"Insanity." Scarlett giggled, but it quickly dissolved into a sob. "Is that your defense, too, Mother?" she asked Ursula. "You left us no choice. We had to fend for ourselves, and then Raphael…" She gasped as if she couldn't catch her breath at the thought of him. "My sweet brother… He's gone. Ripped from this ugly world that has offered us nothing but unrelenting *need*."

"Raphael Lilosa is dead?" Lady Novak asked. Beauclair shot her a murderous glare that made her shrink in her seat. She seemed…*annoyed* that Scarlett had been found—and extra annoyed that Raphael was confirmed dead—but nowhere near resigned. This was only a minor hiccup in her plan.

Ursula had the good sense to shed a tear. As arrogant and stubborn as she'd been, I knew it must have pained her to show any weakness in this flock of vultures. I didn't doubt that her pain was sincere, though I still couldn't understand it. Raphael would always be a soulless heathen in my book.

"Do you deny involvement with the Scarlett Inn?" Beauclair asked, redirecting the conversation.

Scarlett barked out a bitter laugh. "The inn served the downtrodden rejects of your *precious* society. It offered us the comfort and sustenance we were denied—an endless supply of blood and power and…ecstasy." Scarlett closed her eyes and shivered. "More than any vampire could ever want."

Beauclair wobbled on her heels as she took a step back. The ire in her expression was mixed with jealousy and vindictive glee. She was all too pleased with the baroness's confession.

"I think we've heard quite enough," she said. "Is there any councilor here who objects to coffin-locking the former baroness?"

When no one answered, Beauclair nodded to the white cloaks. Scarlett gasped as they wrenched her up out of her chair and dragged her toward the coffin at the back of the stage.

"No!" she screamed. "I'll be good. Mother, don't let them take me!"

She reached out for Ursula as the wardens passed her chair, but the duchess refused to look at her. She sat perfectly still, her shoulders hunched forward, and a haunted look drawing her face tight.

The white cloaks stuffed Scarlett into the coffin and closed the lid on her, while another guard wearing gloves locked the silver bolts and latches in place. Muffled screams and pounding echoed across the theater but soon faded as the coffin was wheeled away.

Beauclair snapped her fingers at one of the guards standing in front of the stage. "Go fetch another coffin," she ordered him. "We're not done here." Then she turned around and folded her hands under her chin, taking in Ursula with a venomous smile. "You're next, Your Ladyship."

Chapter Fifteen

There was something bittersweet about seeing Scarlett stuffed into a coffin. I should have been content that justice had been served—and that I'd *maybe* had something to do with it. But when I thought of everything Scarlett had put Mandy and the other girls at the Scarlett Inn through, coffin-locking just didn't seem like enough.

My hands itched to close around her throat, and a savage pang of regret wormed its way through my heart. I wanted to blame it on my vampiric nature, but I knew I'd feel the same way if my mother's killer had been caught and sentenced to prison.

Lady Beauclair regarded the audience with a snake-oil-salesman smile as they cheered her decision and the council's unanimous consent. Her confidence had faltered when Scarlett arrived, but after putting the exiled baroness away, she looked refreshed. Energized. She was far too enthusiastic about her position to fool anyone into thinking she was here for something as simple or as honorable as civic duty.

The gathered vampires looked more like a mob right now, and I could tell that Beauclair wanted to hurry things along before they fell out of the frenzy she'd stirred them into. She tapped the toe of one stilettoed high heel as she waited for the council wardens to finish setting up the second coffin she'd ordered so she could resume her crusade against the royal family.

Ursula hadn't moved or even glanced up. She looked broken, and while I wanted to pretend that I didn't care if she were stuffed into a coffin the same as Scarlett, some part of me knew that wasn't justice. I wouldn't feel right about it, even if we could hardly stand to be in the same room with one another.

Dante leaned forward and folded his hands in his lap as if in prayer. The corners of his mouth pulled down, and a crease formed between his sympathetic brows. If he'd had wings and were made of concrete, he might have passed for one of those angelic monuments in a graveyard. His gaze flitted to the queen then to the prince before focusing on Beauclair again.

"Ursula Lilosa, Duchess of House Lilith," she boomed in a theatrical voice that made the audience quiver with anticipation. "You are guilty of abandoning two vampling scions who have caused our community a great deal of suffering in your absence. Countless vampires have been coffin-locked for less—"

"Vampires who have not had a noble family to offer their own amends." The queen stood behind the railing of her balcony and stared down at the stage with fire in her eyes. "Do not get ahead of yourself and forget due process, Lady

Beauclair."

"My apologies, Your Majesty." She gritted her teeth and inclined her head no more than an inch. It was the politest insult I'd ever seen. "I was under the impression that the duchess had been disowned along with her criminal scions."

"You are mistaken," the queen replied. "The most Ursula can be accused of is negligence. After the death of her sire, that is understandable. And considering her recent suffering—learning of one scion's death, witnessing another's coffin-locking, and the death of a potential sibling scion—I think she deserves a merciful sentence."

"And what *merciful* sentence would that be, Your Majesty?" Beauclair asked.

"Probationary sirehood."

"Excuse me?"

"Probationary sirehood," Lili repeated. An alarm went off somewhere in the back of my mind as she went on. "I would assign a vampling for Ursula to foster—for half a century—before giving my blessing for her to sire one of her own again. If she fails to adequately mentor the adopted vampling, then I will wash my hands of her and let the council do with her what they see fit."

The audience buzzed excitedly, hushed voices rising and falling as half of their opinions shifted to the queen's line of reasoning, while I tried to convince myself that this was common practice. I was too petrified to ask Dante.

Beauclair scoffed. "We will do what we see fit with her *this* night, Your Majesty."

"I am certain you will." The queen gave the chosen councilors a long, calculating look, pausing on each of them. "I'm simply offering a second solution, my right as head of the accused's house."

"I think it's apparent which solution I find most just." Beauclair smiled sweetly at the queen and tilted her head in faux deference. "No offense."

"None taken." Lili swept out her hand, palm up. "Please, conduct your vote. We eagerly await your verdict."

Beauclair clapped her hands together as she turned back to the seated councilors. "Let us begin with Lord Everett Carter's judgment."

The banker vamp smoothed a hand over his autumn-colored coiffure and buttoned his suit jacket as he stood. His eyes darted around the theater, pausing briefly on the queen, Dante, and then Beauclair. Her gaze narrowed on him, and his nervous smile made me wonder if he were debating whose accounts he could most afford to lose.

"The duchess did not default on her duties without good reason," he finally said. Beauclair's nostrils flared as if she already knew his answer. "Even in banking, we offer grace periods. I vote for probationary sirehood."

One for the home team. Dante wrung his hands in his lap and leaned forward, making sure Lord Carter could see his grateful nod.

"Very well." Beauclair hardly gave him time to sit down before calling on the next councilor. "Lord Bo Starling."

"Probationary sirehood," he answered without standing to explain his decision. The tired tenor of his voice told me that he didn't want to be here. He didn't have anything to gain or lose from the outcome of this trial, and I imagined his household was still grieving the loss of Sonja.

"Lord Owen McCoy?" Beauclair called next, the pitch of her voice sharpening.

Lord McCoy was the least remarkable of the bunch. He stood like Lord Carter had, but he didn't bother buttoning his charcoal jacket. "House Lilith has suffered quite enough in recent years. They are our sovereign leaders, and as such, we should offer them support in this time of need, not hostility."

Beauclair smirked and cocked a hip. "Forgive me, Lord McCoy, but isn't House Lilith your largest account? Perhaps your presence on this council is a conflict of interest."

"House Lilith is not even among my top three accounts." Lord McCoy bristled at the accusation. "If there was a conflict of interest, *Regina*, you should have handled it before calling this trial to order. I vote for probationary sirehood." He sat down with an annoyed huff.

Beauclair's cleavage rose and fell as she fumed, and her face burned nearly as red as her cropped cardigan. She turned her back to the audience to hide her discomposure. "Lord Nicoli DeAngelo," she said, redirecting everyone's attention.

The suave architect beamed at the audience as he stood and folded his hands. His eyebrows drew up in false sympathy, though the look was more genuine on Dante. "It hurts my very soul to think of the two vampling lives lost to such incapable hands." He glanced across the stage to where Ursula sat and shook his head. "I do not believe the duchess deserves the chance to ruin a third. I'm afraid I must vote for the coffin."

Beauclair didn't seem surprised by his vote, though it did restore her poise. "Thank you, Lord DeAngelo. You make a very good point. Lady Wilhelmina Novak?"

The diva fashionista of House Novak had drawn plenty of attention with her lavender hair, but when she stood, all eyes clung to her turquois jumpsuit. The ruffled top looped over one shoulder, leaving the other bare, and the cropped legs revealed a matching pair of heels laced up her calves. She looked like the first flower of spring, and I had to wonder if she was using the trial as an excuse to offer a sneak peek of House Novak's upcoming spring line.

"Members of my household have been coffin-locked for far milder crimes—and for wrongdoings they didn't commit at all," she said, eyeing Lord Starling. Then she scanned the balconies until she found Dante. "Sentences recommended by House Lilith, in fact. Mercy is not something my family was shown. I vote for the coffin."

Three to three.

Dante's hand found mine and squeezed. "This is it," he whispered. "It is all on Louise."

"Does she have anything against House Lilith?"

"Not directly." He winced. "Though she might take issue with the recent slight against House Sorano. They are her largest account."

He was referring to my indiscretions with Roman and the way he chose to handle the situation—which was, somehow, both extreme and merciful. Maybe he thought that balanced the scales. Where I was concerned anyway. It wouldn't help us tonight.

I pressed my lips together and tried to focus on the trial.

"Lady Louise Peyroux," Beauclair called.

The woman stood and regarded Ursula with a sympathetic smile. She placed a hand over her heart and sighed. "I lost my sire to a Dutch assassin before fleeing France," she said, her faint accent intensifying as she shared the memory. "It took some time before I was well enough to join society again. I can't imagine bearing the responsibility of scions and royal duties on top of that suffering. So I choose redemption through probationary sirehood."

"All right, then." Beauclair's smile tightened until it looked more like a grimace. "Thank you, Lady Peyroux," she snapped.

"You're quite welcome," she answered, a silky sweetness to her voice that lacked the backhanded sarcasm Beauclair was laying on thick.

"Probationary sirehood it is." She opened her hands to the audience and hitched her eyebrows as if to say *I tried.*

"By the blood," the crowd answered, though, less enthusiastically than before. Their half-hearted claps were overshadowed by a rumble of disappointed criticism.

Ursula blinked and finally looked up. Confusion clouded her eyes, but I couldn't tell if she knew that she'd just been spared from an extended coffin nap or if she'd simply forgotten where she was.

"However," Beauclair said, hushing the room once again. "I recommend that the council examine the duchess's progress in one year. A mishandled vampling can cause a great deal of damage in very little time. Does any councilor object?" When no one spoke up, she turned toward the queen. "Your Majesty?"

"That's a wonderful idea," Lili said. "Of course, I intend to examine her progress weekly. I have no doubt that the duchess is eager to redeem herself."

Ursula's chin trembled, but she met the queen's gaze with glassy eyes. Then, slowly, her head turned to the other side of the theater, and those eyes locked on mine.

The denial I'd been clinging to evaporated.

"We won." Dante's voice echoed in my head as if we were in a cave.

Did we? I couldn't get myself to say the words aloud.

Anxiety squeezed my stomach until I thought I might regurgitate my evening blood, and red pulsed at the edges of my vision. Someone needed to hit pause. This was all too much. I could hardly focus as Lane fell into step beside me, and we followed Dante upstairs to the queen's suite where Ursula had been taken.

Royal guards and blood donors crowded the hallway in their cloaks, creating a river of red. I spotted Mandy near one of the duke's harem suites. She bounced on her toes, scanning the crowd until her eyes landed on me, and then she was at my side.

"Scarlett?" she whispered.

"Coffin-locked," I answered, still trailing the duke on his way to the queen's suite.

"Then why do you look so pale?"

"Not now." I ground my teeth and pushed past a cluster of donors congregating in front of the prince's and Kassandra's door. I couldn't trust any of them. Not with anything.

Murphy and Donnie hovered near the queen's door, and I guessed that meant the council wardens had turned over Ursula to them. I didn't see any sign of the white cloaks. Dante held up a hand, silently requesting that we wait for him with everyone else as he disappeared inside the queen's suite. When he returned a second later and waved me inside, I couldn't even pretend to be surprised.

My stomach did a little flip-flop as the door closed behind me, muffling the commotion in the hall and giving way to the uncomfortable conversation taking place inside. The entire royal family was present, and it was all I could do not to boldly gawk at Kassandra.

"Please," Ursula begged the queen. "This is a terrible match. She resents me for my scions' crimes."

"*I* resent you for your scions' crimes," Lili said. "Who doesn't?" Her scolding gaze diverted to me, and I bowed my head.

"Your Majesty," Dante said as he ushered me across the room to where they stood in front of the window. "I had hoped to mentor this one myself—in preparation for my own scion."

The queen sighed and gave him a withering look. "Do not think your questionable judgment has escaped my attention. Lord Sorano paid me a visit." Her attention shifted to me, and I again lowered my eyes to the floor and swallowed the bile working its way up the back of my throat.

"I have never been more ashamed of my house," Lili said as though it physically pained her to admit it. After her reprimanding glare, I felt grouped into that category. It wasn't an ideal place to be right now.

"Ursula." The queen tsked the duchess. "You are saved by blood alone this night. You will not find yourself so lucky again."

"Yes, Your Majesty," she answered quietly.

"Alexander, my sweet prince." I stole a glance up to watch as Lili turned and brushed her fingertips under his chin. Kassandra went rigid beside him. A tendon in her neck strained and became more prominent the longer the queen held the prince's attention.

"You raised a strong, independent scion, though I fear you've allowed him to become too willful since shifting focus to your second-born," the queen said as her own focus shifted to Kassandra. "Not that I don't doubt she's required a heavier hand."

Kassandra lowered her gaze, but the tendon in her neck remained rigid. It seemed to amuse the queen, and I wondered if maybe she'd seen more in her would-be assassin's blood than she'd let on.

"Our numbers are compromised," Lili said, waving her hand around the small circle. Then she fastened her eyes on me again, but this time, I couldn't look away. Not while she was sealing my fate. "This vampling saved my life, and for that, I have promised her a sire."

It felt as if my heart were bouncing off my ribs like a pinball machine. An exhilarating nausea seized my stomach as if I were trapped on a rollercoaster. This is what I'd wanted. So desperately that it was the first thing I thought to ask for after I'd saved her life. But she wasn't Santa. *More like Krampus.*

"Ursula will fill the role to atone for her sins, and she will do so at Dante's estate and under his careful observation— since he's so eager to practice for his own scion," Lili said, narrowing her eyes on the duke.

"Yes, Your Grace," he answered automatically. The chore didn't seem to trouble him until she added, "And you will demonstrate everything you've learned when you sire your first next year at Imbolc."

"Your Majesty, I—"

She cut him off with a wave of her hand. "By your age, I had sired both of my children. You have one year. Our family must grow."

Dante slapped a hand to his chest. "I am not ready. *Ursula* was not ready, and look what happened."

The queen closed the gap between them before I could blink. Her hand clamped onto his shoulder, the glossy nail of her thumb grazing the underside of his Adam's apple. Her dark eyes were nearly level with his, and they drank him in with enough intensity that I couldn't find my next breath.

"Our enemies conspire to overthrow us," she whispered. "We lost Morgan to them, and we nearly lost Ursula tonight. There is power in numbers."

"Yes, Your Grace," Dante answered breathlessly.

No one dared mention Scarlett. After her exile and coffin-locking, I guessed she no longer counted as a viable member of House Lilith. I didn't think the queen counted me, officially, either. That left Lili, Alexander, Kassandra, Dante, and Ursula. The whole of House Lilith, in the same room under a foreign roof. Probably not the best place for a family meeting.

The phone in the room rang, and the queen finally released Dante and nodded to the prince to answer it.

"Your car is ready, my queen," he said, covering the receiver with one hand.

Kassandra's face flushed as if she were offended by his affectionate tone. She caught me staring, and her eyes narrowed, sapping the sincerity out of the pathetic smile she offered.

Something told me this was too good of an opportunity for her to pass up. Dante had to suspect the same. He lingered behind as Alexander and Kassandra exited the queen's suite, and then tugged at the hem of my cloak.

"Do not leave Ursula's side," he whispered. "Go with Murphy and have Donnie wait for me with the second car. I'll be along shortly."

I nodded and hurried after the duchess—my new sire.

God help us all.

Chapter Sixteen

Mandy didn't try to grill me again, but I could tell she wanted to. I didn't even know what to say. How was I supposed to tell her that the vampire who had made the lot responsible for so much of her suffering was now my sire?

She'd already packed up my belongings, anticipating—likely praying—that we wouldn't be staying over a second day. We'd only been at the duke's manor for a week and a half, and I never would have guessed that I'd be this eager to return to it. I wanted to close myself up in my room, away from the council and Kassandra. Away from Ursula.

The duchess sniffled as she stuffed her toiletries and robe down into a suitcase. I was waiting for her to order a harem donor to finish the task—or worse, order me to do it. My original vision of being whisked off to London by some dashing vamp to dance the night away was obliterated. The queen had turned my fantasy into a nightmare. A *fifty-year-long* nightmare.

As miserable as I was, wallowing in my self-pity, there was also a twinge of humiliation that I hadn't expected. Ursula seemed even more distraught about the arrangement than I was. As if I were the worst thing that could have happened to her.

"The queen should have let them take me," she said,

more to herself than to me. "She obviously doesn't know the full extent of what she has inflicted."

Ursula zipped her suitcase and forcefully dropped it on the floor beside mine. I jumped, surprised she hadn't taken the opportunity to club me with it. The look she gave me suggested she wanted to.

"I'm not thrilled here either," I snapped. Twitchy nerves made me testy. "You don't exactly have a great track record."

Her hand planted in the center of my chest, and then my shoulder blades bit into the wall behind me. Mandy growled, her eyes going wolfy, but she stayed back a step. This was dangerous territory. Understanding and horror strained her expression, but she wouldn't intervene unless I signaled her to.

Ursula scoffed and shot Mandy a sideways glare. "Go ahead, little wolf," she taunted. "I was ordered to foster this one. Nothing was said about sparing her harem."

"Leave her out of this." I squirmed between Ursula's hand and the wall, trying to free myself. "She's suffered enough because of your incompetence."

Ursula hissed in my face. Her eyes filled with black as her fangs extended. "The duke's leash on you was far too lax, vampling. I will not tolerate your mouth for fifty years. Speak ill of me again, and I will stuff you in a coffin and muzzle your mutt. Do you understand?"

She pressed harder against my chest, sliding my back up the wall until only the toes of my boots grazed the floor. I felt my bones ache in protest. The pistols holstered under my arms were within easy reach, but going for them would spark outright war. I was displeased with the queen's decision. Not suicidal.

"Yes," I rasped.

"And you will address me properly from now on."

"Yes, *Your Grace*."

"That's a good vampling." Ursula released me. I dropped back to my feet and wheezed in a tender breath. "Now call for Murphy. I'm ready to leave this hellhole."

Mandy gathered up our bags to take to the harem's SUV. She gave me a sympathetic scowl and touched my shoulder as soon as Ursula turned her back to us.

"I'll find Murphy, drop off the bags, and then bring the car around," she whispered, buying me some extra time to compose myself. Not that that was likely while in the same room with the duchess.

I nodded, still too breathless to speak. Not that I had anything smart to say—well, nothing *wise* anyway.

Pointing out that I'd helped with her stupid blood call—for whatever good it did—and that I'd agreed to guard duty to keep the council from using me against her wasn't going to earn me any brownie points in her current mood. And I had fifty years of this undead PMS nonsense to look forward to. *Joy*.

Murphy arrived a minute later, and I almost hugged him when I answered the door. My breath finally steadied, and I set my disappointment aside to focus on getting out of there in once piece.

At least half the vampires in the theater had not been satisfied with the council's ruling. Then there were the three council members from fancy, well-staffed households that would have preferred to see the duchess locked away. With Kassandra lurking about, that meant we weren't even safe on the floor reserved for the royal family.

"Donnie's waiting for the duke," Murphy said as we escorted Ursula to the elevators. "And Lane already left with the harem."

I nodded absently, scanning the hallway for threats. Most of the guards and blood donors had cleared out, but a few remained behind—likely the queen's people since Dante was still with her. Donnie stood near the queen's door, his back pressed against the wall. He dipped his head in a small nod when he caught sight of us. Then the elevator door opened, and we loaded inside and headed for the lobby.

Many of the vampires who had attended to witness the trial had remained behind to fawn over the elite council members and the royal family. Ursula tensed as we stepped out into the crowd. Several scathing glances were sent her way, but there were also the odd, over-enthusiastic vamps who called out their support, as well.

"I knew you were innocent all along!"

"True love never dies!"

"Long live Duchess Ursula!"

Ursula's brow pinched, and she urged Murphy and me to hurry, pressing a hand to each of our backs as we tried to navigate the throng. The three sets of double doors that lined the front of the theater stood open, and outside, a sprinkle of snow dotted the night sky, glowing against the lit Gateway Arch in the distance.

The chill of winter filled my lungs, but any relief it might have offered was stunted by Kassandra's smug face. She approached Ursula, and for a moment, I hesitated rather than let her pass. When she turned her viper grin on me, I inched back a step.

"Your Grace," I mumbled as if only just recognizing her. She had enough reason to want me dead. Revealing that I was onto her would only add to that list.

Kassandra took Ursula's hands in both of hers and offered air kisses to either cheek. "Cousin," Kassandra cooed. "It's been too long. Congratulations on the favorable outcome of your trial."

"Thank you." Ursula stared vacantly at the younger

duchess. She'd go through the required motions for the sake of all the eyes glued to her, but she had no intention of embellishing the show. "My car is waiting," she said, ending the conversation before it had a chance to really go anywhere.

"I look forward to visiting more with you at Imbolc," Kassandra said as she stepped out of our path.

Mandy pulled up to the curb a second before we reached the sidewalk. One look from Murphy and she hopped over the console, surrendering the driver's seat to him. I opened the door for the duchess and waited for her to climb inside before circling the car.

As I opened the door across from Ursula's, I stole one last glance at Kassandra. She stood farther down the sidewalk from the mob spilling out of the theater, a cell phone pressed to her ear, expression twisted with thinly veiled rage. Whomever she was speaking to was getting an earful. Her emerald eyes snagged mine, but I quickly ducked into the car.

I knocked on the dark partition glass, cuing Murphy to get us the hell out of there, and we pulled away from the curb and Kassandra's hateful face.

My shoulders felt permanently squared, and it was only half due to my temperamental foster sire sitting on the opposite side of the plush, leather seat spanning the back of the car. Ursula rested her elbow on the armrest of the door and gazed out at the buildings as they blurred past us. The snow swirled against the windows, blown asunder in the car's wake. The moon had already set for the night, but winter seemed to have a blue light of its very own.

This stretch of the city was quiet during the witching hours. We were away from the interstate. The human bars had long since closed, and none of their daytime businesses would be open for some time yet. Only the gentle hum of the car's engine broke the silence.

"I'm sorry."

"What?" I blurted, positive I'd misheard the duchess.

She turned her head, exposing tear-stained cheeks. Her eyes were bloodshot, and they encompassed every emotion on the spectrum. "We got off on the wrong foot, but we have to make this work—for both our sakes."

"It's been a traumatic night," I offered, not quite ready to forgive and forget, but also not ready to start a batfight in the back of a moving car.

Ursula opened and closed her mouth, struggling to find her next words. But before she could get them out, we passed an intersection, and a trash truck plowed through the stoplight—coming right for us.

Chapter Seventeen

Armored cars could take a lot. That's what they were designed to do. Unfortunately, that also meant they lacked crumple zones, so their occupants absorbed the brunt of a crash. Especially if the other vehicle had more mass and weight. A trash truck had quite a bit more of both.

I grabbed the duchess as the truck hit us, dragging her across the seat. We were immediately thrown to the opposite side from the impact, and then my head smacked the ceiling as the car rolled, and the glass partition behind the front seat shattered.

Mandy screamed, but I couldn't reach her. Not while Ursula clung to me and I grasped for anything to hold on to.

The trash truck didn't slow. It pushed us across the street, and I felt another jarring bump as we hit the curb, and the vehicle rolled onto its roof. We landed on a sidewalk that bordered one of the tiny parks tucked in between the buildings.

"Son of a bitch!" Murphy hollered. "My leg is stuck." He was the only one not slumped against the ceiling of the car. His door was caved in all the way to the steering wheel, and his window was spiderwebbed, though somehow still held together by whatever voodoo went into ballistics glass.

My door was scuffed but intact, and through the window,

I watched three men climb out of the trash truck—each wielding an M4 rifle. My blood vision brought them to life in startling detail.

Cruel, rugged faces sneered in our direction. Their massive frames were backlit by the streetlights, casting long shadows over the car. They were dressed in jeans and heavy coats, stocking caps pulled down over their heads. Two of them were unfamiliar, but the third I knew—or at least, we'd met once before. The assassin from Ursula's room at the manor.

"Wolves." Mandy gasped and heaved herself upright, crouching against the roof of the car so she could keep an eye on our assailants through the tinted windows.

"You can smell them through the glass?" Murphy stopped his struggling and gave her a skeptical look. Its intensity was somewhat lost from his upside-down position. His face was red from the rush of blood to his head, and his cloak spilled down to the car's ceiling.

"I recognize them. They're with the Moreau Pack."

"Ursula?" The duchess lay across my back, limp. I tried to be careful as I squirmed and wriggled my way out from under her, but when the wolves opened fire, I gave up and shrugged her off, freeing my pair of Reaper TDs from their holsters.

The windows on our side of the car splintered, shots

randomly peppering the glass. We were up against novices. An expert would have focused their fire until they drilled a hole. Regardless, the windows wouldn't last forever.

I re-holstered one of my guns and ran my hand over the top of the back seat, frantically searching for the lever that would fold them down—or up in our case.

"What are you doing?" Mandy shouted. A growl raked through her voice, and her eyes glowed yellow, lighting up the inside of the car.

"The armored plating will take longer to get through than the glass." My fingers hooked onto a plastic latch, and I pushed the seat up, revealing the dark cave of the trunk. "Help me move the duchess."

Mandy crawled toward me, crunching through the broken partition window. Murphy took the opportunity to stretch across the front of the car and bearhugged her seat, using it for leverage as he kicked his door with the leg that wasn't stuck. It creaked and then flung open as he dropped to the ceiling of the vehicle with a grunt.

"Now we're in business!" Murphy hobbled out— obviously injured and clearly not giving a damn—red cloak flapping behind him like a bullfighter's muleta. I couldn't see this going well at all.

Mandy and I wrangled Ursula into the trunk and pushed the seats back in place. The windows were so battered now that I was sure even if wolves could see through tinted glass, none of them had seen where we'd stashed the duchess.

I crawled toward the front of the car while Mandy stripped out of her cloak and catsuit.

"You can't shift in here," I said. "The glass is about to go." The fire had lessened, thanks to Murphy's departure, but it hadn't stopped.

"Then I'll do it in the park," Mandy snapped.

"Make it quick. I'll cover you."

I yanked off my cloak as I reached the mouth of Murphy's open door. I wasn't as eager to get shot, so I didn't plan on rushing out into the open with a glaring target on my back, but I didn't have much else to work with. And I needed every advantage at my disposal right now.

I balled up the cloak and tossed it over the belly of the upturned car, hoping it would offer enough distraction as Mandy and I made a run for it. I stayed behind her, trying to conceal her pale backside and firing a few rounds at the pair of wolves near the trash truck. I guessed one of them had gone after Murphy.

We neared a cluster of shrubs that bordered a monument, and a round chipped the concrete base, taking a chunk out of it as we hesitated.

"Shit! Shit!" Mandy hissed, clutching her arm. I reached for her, but she waved me off. "It's just a nick. Go. Keep them away from the car."

Bullets zipped through the air between us. Red cloak or not, my blond ponytail was as good a target as any. The gunfire trailed after me as I darted away from Mandy's hiding place. Vampiric reflexes were a definite bonus, but I was still a mere vampling. Dodging bullets was not a skill I had honed.

I drew my second pistol and doubled my fire as I cut through the trees, slipping into the shadows between a pair of parked cars at the curb. My breath fogged, and snowflakes landed on my cheeks and in my hair as shots ripped through metal all around me. A bullet grazed my thigh, and I bit my bottom lip to keep from crying out.

Sirens crooned in the distance. I wondered if they belonged to metro or Blood Vice. Either way, I didn't have time to wait and find out.

I rolled onto my stomach and peered under the car I was using for cover. Something dripped from the motor—fluid from some reservoir or another—and a fast food bag was crushed under one of the front tires. The Eye of Blood illuminated all, but I tried to focus on what mattered.

My breath stilled as the chill of the damp pavement soaked through my bodysuit, sending a shiver through me. I pressed my arms down harder, steadying my aim at the pair of boots drawing closer on the opposite side. Then I fired.

Blood exploded from the werewolf's ankle, and he landed

flat on his back, his gun smacking the concrete beside him. He swore and then loosed a sound that no one would have mistaken for human. I half expected him to shift, but his yellow eyes found me first, locking on mine from beneath the destroyed car. He reached for his M4. Luckily, my pistols were still aimed in the right direction.

I lit him up, none too eager to take a round of 5.56 to the face.

When I was sure he wouldn't be getting back up, I rolled onto my side and swapped out the two Reapers' magazines. My blood vision had faded, but I bit down on the inside of my cheek until I tasted blood, and it returned. Then I crept around the back of the vehicle, scanning the park and crash site.

A shot rang out, and I heard a wolf yelp. My heart throbbed as it pulsed against my breastbone.

Please, don't be Mandy.

A quirky whistle snapped my attention to the upturned car. Murphy squatted behind it. He wagged his eyebrows at me and cocked his head toward the trash truck. I turned in time to see a shadow move between the wheels.

One of the wolves waited on the other side, moving toward the back end. I hurried across the lot on the balls of my feet, stepping lightly as I holstered my pistols. I wouldn't need them for what I had planned.

A large lever angled up from the corner of the truck's bumper. It looked like something a trash guy might use to hang on to while the truck cruised through city alleys. I grabbed it with both hands and pushed off the ground, tucking my knees in against my chest.

The momentum pulled me around the side of the truck as if I were a stripper on a pole. The rifle-toting wolf sucked in an alarmed gasp as my feet planted in the center of his chest, knocking him ass over elbows into the back of the trash truck. His rifle smacked against the bumper and landed in the street.

"Ha!" I shouted, half in victory and half in surprise as the lever in my hand moved.

The mouth of the hopper started to close, crushing bags of trash and corrugated cardboard down on top of the wolfman. He screamed and clawed at the garbage as it compressed around him. I turned away, unable to watch as it finished him off, his cries dissolving with a crunch of bones.

The remaining creep was already moving my way, his rifle taking aim at my head. A bullet whizzed past my face as I reached for my pistols.

"Move!" Mandy yelled through the driver's side window of the truck. Her naked arm poked out, and she slapped her hand against the door impatiently.

I skipped back a step as she threw the truck into reverse

and stepped on the gas, slamming into the man. His last shot echoed inside the hopper of freshly pressed garbage and wolf scum before his rifle went flying across the street. It landed in the intersection just as the duke's car pulled up to the light.

I flagged my arms at Donnie like an idiot. Like maybe he didn't notice the M4 or the banged-up car or the unconscious wolf behind the trash truck. Not to mention the one I'd rendered into hamburger not twenty yards away.

Mandy whooped, and then I heard the unmistakable sound of her shifting. She was still naked, after all. A moment later, her wolf leapt through the truck window.

It was somewhere between three and four in the morning, but a few early birds slowed to gawk at us as they passed by. One parked in a small row of spaces diagonal from the mess we'd made.

"I've called the police," they announced. Their tone was caught somewhere between good Samaritan and tattletale. I hiked both thumbs into the air as I panted, still coming down from the jolt of adrenaline burning up my insides.

Donnie stopped the duke's car in the middle of the street, and the back door opened.

"Ursula?" Dante asked, his wide eyes taking in the carnage and Mandy's wagging tail.

"I've got her." Murphy limped toward us. One of Ursula's arms was slung around his neck, but she was conscious—if a little dazed.

The sirens were louder now, and red lights flickered up from between the buildings. Dante waved his arm for us to hurry.

"Get in," he said, taking Ursula from Murphy. "Blood Vice will intercept, but it would be best if we are not here when the human police arrive—especially considering your history with them," he added in my direction.

He slid across the seat, pulling Ursula along with him until there was room for me. I climbed in and patted my leg for Mandy. Her tongue drew inside her mouth, and her ears lay flat against her head. I couldn't imagine she was thrilled at the idea of lying across the laps of three vamps, but she hopped inside as Murphy dropped into the front passenger seat.

The doors closed, and Donnie pulled away just as two police cars arrived at the scene. I glanced over my shoulder, attempting to see if the human who had called in the incident was redirecting the officers.

"Make it snappy," Donnie said from the front seat. He was on the phone, I realized. Probably with an agent from Blood Vice.

Ursula groaned beside me. A cut sliced across her brow, nearly hidden against her red hairline, but I had a feeling her disquiet had more to do with the wolf in her lap. Mandy's amber eyes slowly turned up to her, and she whined under her breath.

"Trust me," I said. "You don't want her to shift on top of you."

Chapter Eighteen

Yoshiko was waiting in the foyer with a tray containing two blood pots when we returned to the manor. Dante had placed a call to Belinda on the ride across town, relaying our injuries to her, and like a grade-A assistant, she'd set to work making sure we'd be well taken care of upon arrival.

Mandy trotted off to her room to shift as I helped Murphy into a wheelchair. The accident had torn something in his knee—not that he'd let that hold him back in the scrimmage that followed. It was catching up to him now, though. Belinda took the handles on the backrest of his chair and gave me a small smile.

"I have a donor waiting in the gym," she said. Then she patted Murphy's shoulder and turned him toward the north wing. "No stairs for you tonight, big guy."

Dante took Ursula's arm and motioned for Yoshiko and me to follow them down the back hallway that led to his quarters. Dawn was a few hours off yet, so we were taking our morning blood earlier than usual. In our condition, I was sure the harem could forgive us.

"It's werewolf, O-positive." Yoshiko set the tray down on the table near the fireplace. "Should fix you right up, Your Grace," she said to Ursula as Dante deposited her onto one of the stuffed armchairs. He waved a hand at the other, offering it to me.

"You want me to bleed all over your furniture?" I twisted my leg to the side to show him where a rogue round had sliced through my suit. Apparently, the big, bad wolves had been using silver. My thigh was still bleeding. The trail oozed down my calf and disappeared inside my boot. I could feel the tacky moisture soaking into the heel of my sock.

"I'll fetch a towel," Yoshiko said, making for the duke's attached bathroom. She was back in a flash and pressed a terrycloth square into my hand before pouring a round of the werewolf blood for us. "Is there anything else I can get for you, Your Grace?" she asked Dante.

"That will be all. Thank you." He fondly touched her shoulder and bid her a good day, likely out of habit, considering it was still pitch black beyond the sea of windows flanking the fireplace.

Ursula's hands shook as she lifted her cup to her mouth. Under the brighter lighting, I finally got a good look at her head wound. A glimmer of white bone peeked through the crusted blood, and I assumed that a piece of glass from the partition window was to blame. She drank deeply, and the gash contracted, the skin tightening until her skull was once again hidden from sight.

I wasn't so fortunate. Silver left a more lasting mark than glass, as evidenced by the tender, red line over my palm, and while the werewolf blood warmed my core and made my toes tingle, the ragged tear across my thigh would take a few days to fully heal. It stopped the bleeding, at least.

I wiped my leg with the hand towel before taking Dante up on his offer and sitting down next to Ursula, folding my bum leg over the other to avoid staining his fancy chair.

"Any guesses as to whom my secret admirer might be?" Ursula asked as she refilled her cup. She paused before setting the pot down, and then topped off my cup, too. The gesture would have felt more sincere if it weren't so obvious how badly she needed friends right now.

"Those wolves belonged to the Moreau Pack—Mandy recognized them," I added at Dante's skeptical frown. "And one was the assassin who attacked the duchess last week."

"Blood Vice should have them in autopsy soon." He scratched his chin and turned to Ursula. "If I have them send over photographs, do you think you could identify the culprit?"

"Absolutely."

I held up a finger and winced. "We may have a problem. I kind of…sort of…maybe crushed him in the hopper of the trash truck."

Dante shuddered, but Ursula merely cocked an eyebrow.

"It was an accident. Mostly," I added, not sure what to make of their reactions. Was that horror? Awe? Disgust?

"Well, it's not like he didn't have it coming," Ursula finally said. Dante nodded slowly, unable to disagree but still seemingly wigged out by my extreme justice—however accidental. I waited for him to look at me again before I asked what I figured he was wondering himself.

"Kassandra?"

Ursula choked on her blood and covered her mouth with one hand. "What?" she rasped.

Uh-oh. Dante's eyes swelled, and I realized a little too late that he hadn't told her what I'd seen in Emma's blood on All Hallows' Eve. To be fair, he'd agreed to protect my secret— a secret that Ursula had only just discovered the night before.

"She sired the assassin who tried to take out the queen last fall. I bit her, got an Eye of Blood peepshow, and then couldn't tell anyone—for obvious reasons," I said, summing up the short version of the story.

"Except for Dante?" Ursula blinked at him suspiciously.

"Except for Dante," I echoed. Truthfully, I wasn't sure why I'd spilled my guts to the duke. I could have tried harder to keep up the charade, but outing Kassandra to him had made me feel...*safer.*

The duchess's breath grew heavy, and her eyes welled. "You don't suspect that she..."

"We have no proof." The worry creasing Dante's brow made me wonder if there had been another reason he'd kept the information from her. "All we know for certain is that she sired the assassin who attacked the queen. Nothing more."

"But she could have done this," Ursula snapped. "She could be the one responsible for Morgan. And these attacks on me could be her trying to finish the job."

Dante knelt in front of her chair and pulled her hands to his chest. "You cannot let these dark imaginings consume you. We must focus on the task the queen and council have assigned to you in order to mend your reputation."

"What if I can't?" Her breath labored again, and this time she turned her stricken gaze to me. "What if I ruin her the same way I ruined Raphael and Scarlett?"

"Impossible." He shook her hands clasped between his own. "I will be here to assist you every step of the way."

Ursula didn't seem convinced. "What good is that? You've never even *half*-sired anyone."

She wrenched her hands out of his and stood suddenly, pacing across the room to stand before the span of glass overlooking the pool. I knew it was only a matter of time before she had another outburst. She was like a demonic jack-in-the-box. One second consumed by eerie melancholy. The next, an explosion of fury and resentment.

"You are right." Dante sighed and rose to his full height. "But I have read many books on rearing scions, and I have a household full of loyal subjects. That must count for something, cousin."

"You have no need to convince me," she scoffed. "We are bound together by law. The choice is out of my hands."

"Then make your peace with it by Imbolc," Dante said. "And prepare yourself for Kassandra. Whatever else she may or may not be responsible for, she did attempt to murder the queen. She cannot be trusted, but until we have proof and a well-laid trap set for her, we must appear none the wiser."

"You've gotten too good at playing the fool, *cousin*." Ursula turned on her heel and stormed out of the duke's room, slamming the door behind her. Such drama.

"That went well." I finished off my cup of blood, anticipating his dismissal.

Something crashed in the hallway—likely one of the framed sunsets—and Dante snorted. "Swimmingly." Then he shook his head and offered me a weary smile. "Thank you for keeping her safe tonight—for defeating our enemies so...*thoroughly*."

"The one in the truck really was an accident," I said. "And the roadkill victim was Mandy's doing."

"I'll be sure to express my gratitude the next time I see her."

I stood and inspected my leg again, fingering the hole in my suit. "Shark-resistant, huh? Maybe the council could convene at the beach next time."

A dry laugh slipped from Dante. "Let us hope that there is no next time in our near future."

I didn't see Ursula at all the next evening. I wasn't sure if she was avoiding everyone or just me. I didn't care either way. I'd take the peace and quiet while I could get it.

The duke loaned Mandy out to the Cadaver Dogs again, this time for an extended stay through the full moon, and Allen Cable collected her the night before we planned to leave for the queen's Imbolc celebration. I hated being left behind, but I had a *previous engagement*.

Boredom set in quickly when Mandy wasn't around. I'd already packed for the trip to Denver, and I even bit the bullet and *unpacked* a few of my personal possessions stowed in the plastic tubs I'd been living out of. Belinda had found a new shade for my mother's fire hydrant lamp, and though it didn't exactly go with the subtle, feminine theme of the room, the duke seemed pleased when he noticed it on the bedside table.

"Mr. Murphy said you were looking for me?" he said, pausing in my doorway.

"Yes." I crossed the room to the small desk in the corner. It was cluttered with stubs of charcoal and crumpled pages— another attempt to keep my boredom at bay. The drawing I retrieved for him was of the werewolf whose remains now filled a five-gallon bucket in the supernatural morgue under the Blood Vice field office in St. Louis.

"Is this John Wolf number three?" Dante asked, taking in the sketch with a furrowed brow.

"It was the best I could do with how briefly I saw him."

"The detail is striking. I will forward this to Blood Vice for their investigation."

I sighed and bit my bottom lip. "I don't suppose there's any chance that I could *join* the investigation, is there?"

"All in good time, vampling. Let us get through Imbolc first." He nodded his thanks and disappeared down the hall.

Maybe I was reading too much into his apologetic smile, but I wanted to believe him. I couldn't stomach the idea of staying cooped up in this manor for fifty years with the likes of Ursula, and I was having a hard time containing my jealousy regarding Mandy's adventures. Thwarting royal assassins had only whetted my appetite—and I wouldn't be satisfied until I proved who pulled their strings.

I took to the gym to release my frustrations, sparring with Murphy. He teased about a rematch, though we were content to take turns holding the boxing bag for each other for now. His recounting of the trash truck park battle—as everyone had come to call it—seemed to impress the other guards. They had been civil before, but now they regarded me with a new level of respect. I liked it. It made the manor tolerable, but only just.

I still felt as if I were sitting on my hands when I should be out doing something more, like hunting down Arnie Moreau and beating the information we needed out of him. The task sounded so much more productive—and so much *easier*—than playing dress up at some hoity-toity vamp party.

Especially when I didn't know whether or not Roman would be in attendance.

That we'd be in the same city would be hard enough to push from my mind. And even if he didn't show, I had no doubt that *someone* from House Sorano would be there. They were allies of the royal family, and half of an essential partnership that I'd threatened by not keeping my fangs in my mouth. Which made the queen's decision to initiate me into her household extra peculiar. Unless she assumed that House Sorano would see serving under a nightmare like Ursula punishment.

I certainly did.

Ursula was neurotic and reckless and hateful—*and* she had no concept of privacy, as I discovered after returning to my room.

The duchess stood near the desk, her back to me as she flipped through my sketchbook.

"Are you lost?" I threw my sweaty gym towel over my

shoulder and folded my arms.

"I was, but now I'm found. Thanks to *you*." She paused her snooping to smirk at me. "Ironic, isn't it? How you thought bringing me in would buy your freedom. But, instead, it imprisoned us both—together."

"I wasn't trying to *buy* my freedom."

"Oh, no?" She held up the drawing of Roman, seductively reclining in bed, and my breath hitched. "Handsome blood doll, wasn't he? I anointed him a time or two myself back when he belonged to Scarlett and she became a bit...*overzealous*. Or forgetful."

I ground my teeth and glared at her through the thickening screen of my blood vision. If I opened my mouth, I was sure to say something she'd make me regret. To Ursula's credit, she didn't seem to take pleasure in my contained outrage.

"I kept him alive, even when he begged me not to." She turned the sketchpad around to take another look at my rendering of Roman. "The council wouldn't have allowed Scarlett to keep him as a scion. She was but a vampling herself. They would have demanded his ashes—like the one she accidentally turned before him."

I remembered Roman mentioning something about an unsanctioned scion being fed to the sun and delivered to their sire in an urn. What had Scarlett made him endure that he considered true death a better fate?

"I didn't *set out* to create a monster, mind you," Ursula said, carrying on the conversation despite my refusal to be a part of it. "I didn't set out to create *her* at all." She sighed and folded back the cover of the sketchpad, revealing the angry portrait I'd drawn of Raphael.

I braced my shoulders as an unbidden shudder rocked through them, and then I took a step closer, refusing to let her see how much her scion—*my sire*—still haunted me. The Eye of Blood had shown me what a true siring should have been like. The way Lilith had turned Lili, and even the way Kassandra had turned Emma, had been humane. Gentle and with some notion of reverence even.

Raphael had not wanted to sire me. He'd wanted to bleed me dry and burn his *first* illegitimate scion's abandoned brothel down on top of me. And he nearly did. I was an accident. A redheaded step-scion.

"He was…beautiful once." Ursula stroked a finger down the edge of the drawing. "Morgan found him and his sister in the summer of 1915. That was the same year Alexander sired Kassandra. Raphael and Scarlett were being sold off by their parents. They could no longer afford to feed them—thanks to the new child labor laws that saw their factory hours cut in half. Morgan was such a bleeding heart, and Scarlett had a sympathy-inducing way about her."

"Yeah, a real gem," I grumbled and finally mustered up enough nerve to snatch the sketchpad away from Ursula. "She was bait, trap, and hunter all in one."

Ursula nodded slowly, and her eyes unfocused as she stared off into space. "She had a taste for blood from the very beginning. I caught her drinking from my harem more than once—as a *human*. I had her and the blood doll whipped for their insolence, of course."

"Oh, of course."

She went on, unfazed by my sarcasm. "Scarlett was disobedient and difficult, but there is no denying that she was also a powerful vampire. I first anointed her on her sixteenth birthday. She was crafty for a young human, and she only grew more formidable as a half-sired fledgling."

A knock at the door interrupted story time, and I considered making a run for it. I really couldn't care less about Ursula's hell spawns' formative years. The duchess was a shitty sire. We'd already established that. What more did she think I needed to know?

One of the harem donors poked his head inside the room, a tray with a blood pot and two espresso cups tucked in the bend of one arm. "You requested blood for two, Your Grace?"

"Yes, thank you." Ursula crooked a finger at him.

The poor guy shot me an uncomfortable, apologetic

grimace as he crossed the room and set the tray down on the desk. This was my little corner of the manor, and the only other person I'd tolerated ordering people about in my space was the duke—and that was only because he owned the damn place. But my attention shifted before I could call Ursula out on the offense.

"Blood for *two*? Is the duke joining us?"

Ursula rolled her eyes and sat on the edge of my desk. "It's for you. I'm *trying* to be a decent sire here. Consider this our practice round before we have to face the queen again."

I swallowed, remembering that the daunting reunion was just two nights away, and pulled out the desk chair to sit down.

"Okay, sure—*I mean*—thank you, Your Grace." I picked up the pot of blood and filled one of the cups, handing it to her before reaching for the second. Ursula waited until my drink was poured and then clinked her tiny cup against mine.

"See?" she said. "This isn't so bad. Now, where was I?"

I took a swallow of my blood, hoping it would pacify my hangry annoyance long enough to suffer through the rest of her creep-tastic tale. "I think you were about to get to the part where you turned Raphael, and Scarlett decided to help herself to his blood, too."

Ursula's bottom lip crumpled, and she looked away as she took a sip from her cup. "I should have been firmer with her. She was too willful and required a much heavier hand than I employed at the time. If I'd been a better sire, Scarlett would have excelled as a royal scion."

"I think some people just aren't meant to be vampires. It wasn't your fault that she was batshit crazy." I didn't know why I was trying to comfort her, but I guessed it wasn't a bad start if I were going to be stuck with her for years to come.

"It *was* my fault." Ursula lifted her cup again and took a longer drink. Blood coated her top lip, and she licked it clean with a thoughtful frown. "I could have molded her into the perfect vampire, and instead, I abandoned her to wallow in my own grief. I won't do the same to you. I won't let Morgan down again."

The promise sent a chill through me.

I needed facts, not molding. All this talk of whipping and heavy hands…if she thought that shit was going to fly with me, we were going to have problems. I was peeved enough with her snooping through my things.

"You stink," Ursula said, twitching her nose at me. She set her empty cup down on the tray and hopped off my desk. "Finish your blood and rinse off. The tailor will be here in twenty minutes."

"Tailor?"

"We're being fitted for our Imbolc dresses. Chop-chop, vampling." She clapped her hands in my face. "I expect my new scion to wow the masses."

I cradled my cup of blood to my chest and blinked after her as she left my room.

Yep. This punishment was definitely a dual sentence. Two bats, one stone. The queen was teaching us both a lesson.

I just hoped we'd survive it.

Chapter Nineteen

The entirety of the next night was spent in an armored car cutting across the Midwest. Dante had dispatched three sets of decoy vehicles the night we left for Denver, sending them off in various directions. Though, I had a feeling that our enemies would require more time to regroup after the park debacle.

We arrived unscathed, and the queen's staff tucked us in for the day, our last reprieve before the party—and the ceremony that would make the union between Ursula and I *official*. If the anticipation didn't kill me first.

Murphy bowed and held out his hand to me as we entered the foyer of the queen's house. "Your Ladyship," he said, a quiet note of humor in his voice.

I tried not to scowl as I slipped my sweaty palm into his and scanned the ballroom like a desperate teenager at prom. At least I didn't look the part.

Ursula knew a thing or two about dressing for fancy parties. Sure, she'd been out of the loop of vamp high society for a while, but that's what high-end stylists and tailors were for. My airy, chiffon gown was a dusty rose color, and I hated to admit it, but the damn thing was actually comfortable. A professional hair and makeup artist had curled and pinned and painted me until I resembled a porcelain doll, and Ursula had spritzed me with some fruity perfume before we left our guest suite.

Dante seemed to be the only one not interested in forcing us to be roomies. *Thank goodness.*

The duchess had decided that we should take a walk through the back gardens until more guests arrived—because what fun was being introduced to an empty room? And now we were ready to make our debut.

The doorman didn't bother announcing me—who was I, anyway? But he perked as Ursula entered through the double doors at my back. She'd chosen a green gown for herself, similar in style to mine, with the flowy chiffon and petal-like sleeves. Donnie and Lane stood a few steps behind her, wearing white tuxedo jackets and black pants, same as Murphy.

Technically, I was on bodyguard detail, too. But the dress and all the glitz set me apart from the guys. Though, it also made our little entourage look less standoffish. Murphy released my hand and moved in behind us with Donnie and Lane, forming an impenetrable wall at the duchess's back.

"Her Grace, Ursula, Duchess of House Lilith," the doorman declared to the crowd congregating in the mouth of the ballroom. Now that Ursula was sharing the title with Kassandra, they would be announced by first name, as well.

The din of the crowd dropped off suddenly as everyone turned to watch her enter—and by proximity, watch me enter, too. If there were any question about whom the queen would assign as Ursula's adoptive scion, our stylistic twin treatment erased all doubt.

My face warmed as the stares lingered, some inquisitive and others envious. How many of these fanged rubbernecks were our foes? How many were harmless critics? Could *any* of them be trusted? I hoped the makeup hid the worst of my discomfort.

"Smile," Ursula said under her breath, her face frozen in a mask of muted gratitude. I assumed it was the most extreme expression she had decided she could fake for the duration of the party. It wasn't too over the top, but it seemed to pacify the mob of bloodsuckers.

I tried to mirror the look, but even the smallest effort made my cheeks ache after more than a few seconds. I was out of practice. Smiling pretty was Laura's specialty.

Lord Starling was the first to greet us as we ventured deeper into the ballroom. A young man in a similar Kung Fu getup was at his side, and it occurred to me that maybe Ursula's twin fashion was an Imbolc custom. There were dozens of matchy duos scattered throughout the room.

"Your Grace," Lord Starling said, placing a hand over his heart and dipping his chin politely. "I never got the chance to offer my condolences."

Ursula touched his hand. "I didn't either. How is Tabitha?"

"She is struggling," he admitted, then nodded to the man beside him. "Merlin was pledged to become her second tonight, but she is in no condition to mentor a new scion. Still, House Starling cannot afford to forfeit the opportunity to grow, so I shall take him as my fifth. These bonds are sacred and should not be forced."

I wasn't sure if he was referring to the bond Ursula and I had been ordered to forge, or maybe the ones she'd shared with Scarlett and Raphael. Either way, she didn't offer him anything more than a placid smile. A proper duchess did not openly decry the queen's demands.

Tabitha had to be Sonja's sire. The only vampire I'd made friends with at the bat cave—until the last few weeks, anyway. Though, I didn't quite consider the rest of my training unit *friends*. More like cordial acquaintances.

I heard Blair Hanson's familiar chortle over the crowd. She stood on the opposite side of the ballroom near the hall that led to the art gallery. Mic was with her, keeping a careful eye on the House Starling guests. He caught my gaze, and his mouth softened into a weak smile. It was far more pleasant than the sneer he'd perfected during our three months of training.

Mic hadn't forgotten who freed him from the coffin he'd been sentenced to after being falsely accused of Sonja's murder. His house was still bitter over the slight, but at least I didn't have to worry about *him* holding it against *me*.

Lord Starling cleared his throat, and I returned my attention to him.

"Tabitha will be pleased to hear that your adoptive scion helped apprehend Sonja's killer." He made it sound so...*professional* and clean, when the event itself had been anything but.

"Yes," Ursula cooed. "She is quite extraordinary. The queen flatters me with such a *gem*."

My ears burned. The duchess had been referring to me as a diamond in the rough since we'd struck our uneasy truce. Her new determination was unnerving, to say the least.

"Cousin," Dante called as he slipped through the crowd.

He'd arrived at the party before us to speak with the queen about his scion candidates, so I hadn't seen his evening attire yet. The shimmery blue three-piece suit was a work of art. I openly admired him and could hardly suppress a laugh when he blushed. As if every woman in the room weren't looking at him the same way.

"Forgive me for interrupting, Lord Starling," he said to the older vampire.

"Not at all, Your Grace."

Dante straightened the lapels of his jacket. "Shall we prepare for the ceremony?" he said to Ursula and me, holding out an arm to each of us.

I hooked my hand inside the bend of his elbow, mirroring Ursula on his opposite arm. Anticipating and copying her moves seemed to minimize the nitpicking. The extra effort was vital if I wanted to preserve my sanity.

Guests curtseyed or tipped their hats at the duke and duchess as we headed for the queen's receiving room. I felt like an awkward third wheel, but when I attempted to withdraw my hand from Dante's arm, he pinned it between his elbow and ribcage.

"Thirty-six scions will be presented to the queen this year," he said. "You will be first in line."

"Thirty-six?" Ursula made a pained face. "Must we stay for the full ceremony?"

"Considering your need to reaffirm alliances, it would be advisable."

She groaned softly but didn't object.

"Is Kassandra here yet?" I asked. Saying her name aloud rose a bead of sweat along my hairline. I'd ruined her big plans to take out the queen, and now we were going to be fam. Sort of. She had to be just as *thrilled* about it as I was.

"No," Dante answered with a grin. "Let her be fashionably late while we remain one step ahead."

The throne room had been rearranged since the All Hallows' Eve ball. It was lined with rows of high-back chairs decorated with colorful ribbons. White curtains hung from the walls, and they seemed to reflect the light until it created a blinding brightness that made my eyes water.

The queen's ornate chair was angled off to the left side of the dais along the back wall, and five smaller, but equally decorated chairs were lined up at the opposite end.

Ursula groaned again. "She *would* put my damn chair on the stage, wouldn't she?"

Dante pressed his lips together and gave her a tight smile. "Did you really expect her to make this easy? Play nice and restore her trust in you."

I followed them, stopping at the edge of the dais to glance at the reservation cards in the front row.

"Who are you looking for?" Dante asked. He'd released my hand and now stood in front of the center chair of the five opposite the queen's. Ursula took the one to his left.

"Uh, myself?" I cocked an eyebrow. "Who else would I be looking for?"

"You're up here with me." Ursula patted the empty chair at the end of the row and rolled her eyes. "You're going to be my scion. Why would you sit anywhere else?"

I didn't know what to say. It seemed beyond awkward to be grouped in with them, but I climbed the platform stairs and took the chair she directed me to without further comment.

I supposed the remaining two chairs were for the prince and Kassandra. I practiced my poker face on the guests as they began trickling into the room, hoping I'd have it down before the royal scourge arrived.

"Breathe in, breathe out," Ursula crooned in my ear. "The trick isn't to pretend you're a statue—it's to imagine you're alive. Smile. Nod. Laugh a little as though you haven't a care or worry in the world."

"I might have too many of those to make this work."

"Not tonight you don't, vampling." She patted the top of my hand where it lay on the armrest of my chair. "It's Imbolc. Time to focus on cleaning slates and starting fresh."

"If you say so."

"I do."

The room filled up quickly, the hum of chattering guests drowning out my thoughts. I was thankful for the mild chaos. It made it easier to avoid Kassandra's glare when she arrived with the prince. Her pastel yellow gown matched the prince's suit jacket. They looked like a pair of daffodils swaying in the breeze as they paused every few feet to greet guests.

I stood with Ursula and Dante as the pair reached the stage, a courtesy they accepted with small bows before taking their designated seats.

The queen arrived very last with a dozen decorated guards swarming around her like bees on a full bloom. She wore a gown that would have made any bride swoon—layers and layers of white silk and tulle, pearl beads and lace. It was a wonder she could fit down the center aisle and walk up the stage steps, but she did. And she pulled it off like a boss. I wondered how many hours of practice that had taken to nail down.

When Lili reached the dais, she turned and opened her arms to silence the crowd. "Tonight, on the sacred eve of Imbolc, we welcome home my grandscion, Ursula. Her return fills a void that our community has felt since the death of my firstborn, Morgan, and Ursula brings with her a vampling of remarkable prestige, an orphan who has gone above and beyond to serve the call of her kin. May Selene bless their bond and heal their hearts as well as our own."

"By the blood!" everyone cheered.

Lili basked in their praise and then turned to us. "Tonight, my children, you are born anew. Rise, Ursula, Princess of House Lilith, and anoint your new scion for your kin to bear witness."

A collective gasp stirred in the crowd. My own was added to the mix. No one had mentioned anything about bumping her up to princess.

I stole a glance behind us to where Kassandra sat beside

the prince. Her face was unreadable, but that telltale tendon in her neck was at it again. Alexander's surprise was plainer, his eyes blinking stiffly, mouth parted in a small *o*.

"Jenna," Ursula whispered, drawing my attention as one of the servants approached with the shiny tray that held the queen's ceremonial dagger.

We'd gone over this part at least. I lifted the chiffon skirt of my dress and knelt at Ursula's feet—at the *princess's* feet. She seemed surprised herself. In fact, the one who didn't look completely blown away, other than the queen, was Dante. I wondered if he had conspired with the queen and helped orchestrate this grand reveal, and what advantage he thought it provided.

Ursula's hands shook as she collected the dagger from the tray. It was already unsheathed, leaving her other hand free for the bleeding. She angled the tip over her index finger, but it took her a moment longer to steady her aim before she pressed the blade to flesh.

A dark drop of blood rose to the surface. It swelled on her fingertip, quickly nearing the point where it would break and run. My mouth opened automatically, anticipating her next move. I was a fast learner when I applied myself. But Ursula hesitated.

She knew how the Eye of Blood worked. The secrets it would lay bare. She'd taken my blood by force, the same way her scion had taken my life, and only now did I recognize her shame and regret. Her blue eyes brimmed with tears as they searched mine, and she took a timid breath before finally pressing the tip of her finger to my tongue.

"With this blood, I anoint thee mine forevermore." Her voice was little more than a whisper, but it echoed through my head, harmonizing with another.

The vision, while the tamest the eye had revealed, was also the most jarring. It took place in a room much like the one we were in now, and with many of the same guests watching. Morgan stood where Ursula had been a moment before, dark hair unraveling over both shoulders, her hazel eyes ripe and filled with longing.

Blood trickled from a cut on her finger, but as she reached to touch it to my tongue—to *Ursula's* tongue—once more, the queen cleared her throat. This was a public ceremony, not a bedchamber. The groom did not take his bride at the altar, nor reveal whatever taboo practices they enjoyed in private.

"Come, my love."

I felt Morgan's hand on my elbow as she helped Ursula to her feet. They fled the throne room, giggling as they stumbled through halls lit with flaming chandeliers and into a dark room. Morgan's arm circled my back, and her lips grazed my throat as we fell back onto a canopied bed. The pain hardly registered when she bit down. Everything else felt so *good*.

My heart fluttered and ached. It beat too fast. Like a hummingbird's. I couldn't remember ever feeling this alive as a human—but Ursula had. And she'd given it all away for a love she'd thought would last an eternity.

Chapter Twenty

Ursula's finger was still in my mouth when the queen cleared her throat. The new princess returned the dagger to the serving tray and helped me stand. She might as well have been stuck in the vision with me. Her cheeks colored, and she avoided my gaze.

"Welcome, Jenna, Duchess Tempus of House Lilith," the queen said.

I nearly tripped over the hem of my dress as the crowd cheered, "By the blood!"

What the hell was a *duchess tempus*? And why hadn't someone explained it to me before I was declared one?

I trailed after Ursula, back to our seats at the other end of the queen's dais, and tried to snag her attention as the next sire-scion pair was called forward. Her hands gripped the armrests of her chair, and her breath was uneven, but she soon composed herself to focus on the ceremony.

My questions would have to wait. I tried not to fidget as the time crawled by, but *man*. It was hard.

Anytime my knee bobbed, or I stuck a finger in my mouth to chew a nail, Ursula would shoot me a warning glare that made my skin crawl. Pretending to be living rather than imitating a statue apparently meant something different around here.

When the festivities finally wound down, and we were dismissed, Ursula bolted ahead of me toward our suite.

"Wait up!" I called after her.

She spun around and huffed at me. "I just…I just need a few minutes alone. Can you allow me that much, Jenna?"

My mouth dropped open. I was shocked that she even bothered to ask. "Yeah. Right. Of course."

"Thank you." She disappeared into the suite, closing the door behind her.

"She'll come around." Murphy's voice startled me, and I sucked in a surprised breath. He, Donnie, and Lane took up posts in the hallway. The party was over, and bodyguard duty had resumed. Dante appeared soon after them.

"Come, take a walk with me," he said, eyeing the closed suite door.

"I'm supposed to be guarding the princess."

He nodded to the guards stationed in the hall. "I think they can manage without you for a few moments. Besides, the day shift will be arriving shortly."

I frowned at Murphy's teasing grin. He was sure to give me hell about this the next time we sparred.

"Fine." I folded my arms and followed him away from the suite, suddenly wishing I had been given my own. I hadn't expected to feel so needy where Ursula was concerned.

Dante crossed his hands behind his back and nudged my

shoulder with his. "Do you still hate me?"

I tilted my head from side to side as if giving the question serious consideration. "Hate's a strong word."

"But is it an accurate one?" he asked. "We are going to be stuck with each other for at least fifty years. Would it not be more enjoyable and beneficial if we passed that time as friends?"

"Friends?" I tried out the word with him in mind. It felt...odd.

A week ago, I'd wanted to choke the life out of him. I thought he was to blame for everything wrong in my life. Now, I was an honorary member of the royal family and destined to live under his roof for the next fifty years. Maybe he wasn't out to ruin my life, after all.

"Friends," I said again, more thoughtfully.

"Could we not all use more of those?" His eyebrows hitched up in the center, giving him that sympathetic look that I'd found so disarming when we first met. It defused me now again, melting the edges of the ice that encased my broken heart.

"I'm not a very good friend to have," I confessed. "Too many enemies, I'm afraid."

"Well, as an enemy of your enemies, I only see that as one more reason to cement our friendship."

We passed a large, framed print of a setting sun, and I

paused to nod at it. "One of yours?"

"It is."

"What is it about dusk and dawn with you?"

Dante's smile widened, and he loosed a soft laugh. "That is where the magic happens, is it not? When we die and when we are reborn. I suppose it fascinates me—how our souls flee from the sun's light." He glanced up at the photograph. "Do you like it?"

"It's nice." The compliment had sounded better in my head. "I really like the one in my room, with the purple and pink sky."

"That one is my favorite. I captured it over the lake behind the manor years ago."

We continued down the hall a few steps until I stopped and turned to him again. "Did we just have a conversation that wasn't about a dark family secret or attempted assassination?"

"I believe we did, Your Ladyship."

"Does this mean we're friends now, Your Grace?"

He grinned. "I think it is a fine place to start."

Catch up with Jenna and company in…

BLOOD, SWEAT, AND TEARS
BLOOD VICE BOOK SIX

Available Now!

Jenna Skye, the new Duchess Tempus of House Lilith, is losing her mind. After spending eight months holed up in the duke's manor with her new sire, the slightly nutty and ever moody Ursula, all she wants to do is to get out of the house. She'll take any excuse she can to ditch the princess's etiquette lessons and do something worthwhile with her time—even if it means visiting a fancy blood finishing school where one of Dante's potential scions has gone missing.

Jenna's sudden jealousy forces her to take a closer look at the conflicted feelings she has for Dante, and the guilt she still harbors over Roman Knight's fateful farewell. Of course, a house full of new residents, preparations for the upcoming All Hallows' Eve ball, and unsolved murders don't leave much time for introspection.

ACKNOWLEDGMENTS

Thanks to all the usual peeps who help me make these books happen: Chelle Olson, my epic editor, who works so hard to make my words pretty (even when I miss deadlines—sorry!); Rebecca Frank, who designed another lovely cover, this one featuring the epic Gateway Arch; my cover model, a.k.a. little seester, who knows how to strike a pose; Hollie Jackson, who brings Jenna's voice to life in the audiobooks; my critique group, the Four Horsemen of the Bookocalypse, who are always supportive and inspiring; THE Professor George Shelley, for proofreading my books—even though I've strayed from Limbo City; my sweet son, who reminds me of the importance of taking a break every now and then to watch *The Little Mermaid* and eat popcorn with him; my husband, who once again kept everything from going to hell in a handbasket while I panicked over fleeting deadlines; and all my Grim Readers, who take time to send encouraging emails, leave reviews, and hang out with me on online. You guys rock!

ABOUT THE AUTHOR

USA Today bestselling fantasy author **Angela Roquet** is a great big weirdo. She lives in Missouri with her husband and son in a house stuffed with books, toys, skulls, owls, and glitter-speckled craft supplies. She's a member of SFWA and HWA, as well as the Four Horsemen of the Bookocalypse, her epic book critique group, where she's known as Death. When not swearing at the keyboard, she enjoys boating with her family at Lake of the Ozarks and reading books that raise eyebrows. You can find Angela online at **www.angelaroquet.com**

If you enjoyed this book, please leave a review. Your support and feedback are greatly appreciated!